THE HAPPIEST COUPLE IN THE WORLD

AMY D'ORAZIO

Quills & Quartos
PUBLISHING

Edited by Jan Ashton

Cover by James Egan, Bookfly Design

ISBN 978-1-956613-21-6 (ebook) and 978-1-956613-22-3 (paperback)

For my own little bambinos

CONTENTS

It is settled between us already, that we are to be the happiest couple in the world

—ELIZABETH BENNET
PRIDE AND PREJUDICE (CHAPTER 59)

PROLOGUE

The letter from Derbyshire had been read and studied dozens of times. Fitzwilliam Darcy was not a gambling man, but as it seemed he was about to embark on a wager of high stakes, it would have to be thoroughly considered. This gamble in particular was one he could not lose. He had spent night after night in contemplation of it, this unholy jumble in which he would, willingly, entangle himself. Like his wife had before him, he had come to see they had run out of options for themselves and for Pemberley; unlike his wife, he believed salvation could have a different hue.

The day after he had reached his decision, Darcy alit from his carriage, taking a moment to examine the neighbourhood in which he found himself. It was as he might have imagined: a place where one could get the maximum degree of respectability for a minimum price. He had no doubt, were he to knock door to door, that he would find the homes he saw filled with shopkeepers on their way up or gentlemen's daughters and widows on their way down. The neighbourhood did have the advantage of being rather near the park, which he imagined was vastly appealing to one who had been raised in the fresh air of the country.

He had sent his card in with his coachman, who returned with the lady herself. He supposed he could not be entirely surprised she did not have a housekeeper —it was that sort of place. Her eyes were wide, but her dress and her person were tidy. She seemed a little fearful—surely not of him?

"Mr Darcy?"

He bowed, giving her a truncated gesture of respect. "May I come in?"

She cast a glance around at the street, no doubt wondering which of her neighbours might see her admitting a gentleman caller. Ironic, considering the situation they found themselves partnered within. "Yes, please do," she said hurriedly. He closed the door behind him as he followed her in.

Almost as if she had read his thoughts, she said, over her shoulder, "You likely think me very silly to be concerned about my reputation, given our...our arrangement."

"Not at all, I assure you."

"Old habits die hard, I suppose."

"I daresay they do."

She led him to a parlour that was small but neat and

charmingly decorated in the manner of a woman who lived alone. A well-worn chair in some indeterminate hue was drawn very near the fire, and abundant floral pillows lay scattered about the room. A novel rested, open, on a nearby table, and a sewing basket, with a long, white stocking dangling from it, sat on the floor by the comfortable chair. She noticed it at the same time he did and flushed a becoming pink as she hastened to tuck away that which she had been mending.

As he watched her do so, he considered, as he had not before, that she was a very attractive woman. His initial impression had been different, but that, he knew now, was more a result of his discomfort than the actual truth of it. She was very handsome indeed, and witty and clearly good-hearted. In all, an ideal partner in perjury.

"Would you like some tea?" she asked.

In deference to her likely straitened finances, he declined, though in truth, tea might have done him some good. Tea was needed when one had to speak of such things as this. Instead, he asked for water, or barley water, whichever she had on hand. She went to get it.

"I have someone come in to help me in the mornings," she said when she returned with the glass. "I do not, as a rule, have many callers, so I have no need of her above that."

"No, no, think nothing of that," he said hastily.

"When I think of how many servants my father's house had!" She laughed politely. "It seems an unspeakable luxury, but then again, for just me it would be vastly foolish, not to mention quite beyond my touch."

He had not before been much interested in knowing

about her family—clearly they had either been sunk as she had or had passed away—but now asked politely after them all. She answered in similar accents, obviously knowing he had not come to her to speak of such commonplace things.

At length, he set aside the barley water she brought him, leant towards her, and said, "No doubt you are wondering what brings me here to you."

She went very still. Her eyes wide, she nodded. "I do indeed, sir. I believed we had understood all...that everything was...was settled?"

"It will not do." With a deep breath, he shook his head. "No—I simply cannot even consider that which my wife... I love my wife far too much to..." Humiliation cast a hot flush over him, and he prayed she would come to his rescue without him having to speak it outright.

She was disappointed. He did not flatter himself to think that had anything to do with him, only the money. "I understand. So you wish to terminate the arrangement?"

"No."

"No?"

He pressed his lips together a moment then said, "There is something else I require of you, something that is perhaps quite different than what you may expect. Allow me, if you will, to explain."

CHAPTER ONE

THE PRUDENCE OF THE ALLIANCE

April 1817

I t was never easy to be at Rosings Park. Lady Catherine had never quite forgiven him for failing to marry Anne, who, now one-and-thirty years of age, remained unwed. Lady Catherine kept a watchful eye on Elizabeth, always seeking an error, a misstep of any sort which would confirm to herself that Darcy had erred in his choice of a wife.

And the fright of it all was that he was beginning to think he had. He had once believed that a marriage rooted in ardent love could only bring the greatest felicity; alas, he had learnt it could also result in the greatest pain.

Sitting in the drawing room after dinner, having

played the requisite rubber of whist, Darcy considered his wife. She sat across from him on a small sofa next to Anne, murmuring to her about something. Whatever resentment Lady Catherine had about his marriage, it was not shared by Anne, who had become friends with Elizabeth. Indeed, for Anne alone, Elizabeth often said she anticipated their visits to Rosings.

When the clock struck the hour, Elizabeth said something to Anne, and both ladies rose. "I believe I shall retire," Elizabeth announced. "We are off at first light. Are we not, Darcy?"

"Yes," he said, and without looking at him, she quit the room. He knew better than to imagine he should join her in her bedchamber later. Lady Catherine had continued putting him up in bachelors' quarters, a fact they had laughed about in the early years but which now seemed premonitory.

He had just risen to go up himself when Lady Catherine, unexpectedly, said, "Darcy, have a glass of Green Chartreuse with me."

There was a side of Lady Catherine that few knew, a side rarely shown to anyone. Long before she had become the grand lady of Rosings Park, Lady Catherine had been something of a scapegrace. She had enjoyed gambling and strong drink, and she would sometimes gallop through Hyde Park at a breakneck pace. The old earl, Darcy's grandfather, had married her off to Sir Lewis de Bourgh, hoping Sir Lewis would settle her down, but then Sir Lewis had gone off and died instead. The young widow de Bourgh was left with an estate in arrears and a babe in the cradle. That along with Anne's subsequent illnesses and difficulties had tamed Lady

Catherine but had also soured her high animal spirits into ill humour.

But she still enjoyed a good stiff drink now and then.

"Where did you come upon Green Chartreuse?" Darcy asked her with a chuckle.

"Never you mind that," she said, laying one finger alongside her nose. She summoned a footman to bring them their drinks and beckoned her nephew into a chair closer to the fire. For awhile, they merely watched the fire and chewed over matters of little consequence—the recent, difficult birth of a horse in Rosings's stables and whether they thought the summer might bring drought. It was not until his eyes had begun to droop that she brought up the true object of her interest.

"What shall you do about Pemberley?"

He was suddenly wide awake, on his guard, though outwardly he remained impassive. "In the case of a drought? We shall do as we always do and—"

"Darcy." She peered at him over the line of her long, aristocratic nose. "I am talking about your wife's inability to give you an heir."

The usual denials rose to his mind—'we are still young,' 'there is time'—but instead he found himself sighing heavily and admitting, "I do not know."

After a measured pause, Lady Catherine offered, "I know of an excellent midwife. She has been of use to Lady Metcalfe's sister."

"We have seen a dozen midwives and physicians and apothecaries. Nothing has helped."

He might have expected Lady Catherine to begin one of her harangues, her well-intentioned but officious advice. If she had, it would have been easier to set his guard up; instead, she reached over, laid her hand on his arm, and squeezed with gentle reassurance. "I am sorry, my dear boy."

Such simple words, but they nearly laid him low. He was required to swallow and take another drink before he could admit, "Things have certainly not turned out how I had imagined."

"It puts a strain on a marriage," Lady Catherine said. "Trust me, well do I know, and Rosings had no entail. Anne was just as good as a son from that angle."

"A daughter or a son would make my joy complete, but it seems neither is to be."

"The disappointment has made your wife grow quite dull, but at least her country-town indifference to decorum has been checked."

He ignored the last and said, "She is not dull; she is melancholic."

"And you are resentful and angry at her for failing you."

"No, no," he demurred. "Not that."

Her silence penetrated his defences, and he, after a glance at the door, said, "How could I resent her for it, when it is not her fault?"

"I suppose what they have always said about these country girls is not true after all."

"I daresay it is not—not in our case, at any rate."

"And Pemberley will then go to your cousins? Those Darcys up in Warwickshire, is it?" She sniffed. "Sorry lot they are. They are like to run it into the ground."

Darcy protested that assertion half-heartedly. "They are not bad folk, and in any case, it would be my uncle's grandson to inherit—Cooper Darcy, presently aged fourteen and at school."

"Cooper?" Lady Catherine raised a brow. "What sort of name is Cooper?"

"His mother's people, I daresay, and you are looking at the wrong man if you think that is strange."

She chuckled. "One cannot deny that. Well, you should perhaps have the boy to Pemberley for some months. Perhaps this summer." Lady Catherine set her glass down on the side table with a firm thump and rose.

Darcy rose with her, agreeing with her action if not her words. Some foolish part of him, it seemed, yet had hope. Accursed, wretched hope.

An hour or so later, he lay awake in his bed. His bed, not theirs—it had not been *their* bed for some time. His mind was busy mulling over that which it had brushed against lightly before: Had marrying his beloved made him a happier husband? Or a more miserable one?

He could still remember, vividly, those walks in the groves of Rosings wherein he had decided that a staid marriage of practicality was not for him. He had been determined that he should have love. He would have felicity, companionship, passion, and romance for the remainder of his days, side by side with his beloved Elizabeth. With foolish naivety, he had believed it would be easy. Two hearts, two minds, two souls would become as one and live in harmony forever after.

It had not quite worked out that way. No, the Elizabeth he wanted, the woman he had yearned for so desperately in those days, was long gone. In her place was a woman he knew less and less with every passing day, and it pained him. He found himself in a marriage much like the one he had dreaded, the one he believed he had avoided—a marriage marked by strained dinner conversation, tiresome on-dits, and a far-too-frequent, desperate wish to simply be alone. Sometimes he thought it would have been easier to have loved her less; he never could have repined the loss of something that never was.

Worse yet, there was nothing for it. He had tried everything to fix it. God knew he had. He had tried spending more time with her, until it became clear she did not wish for it. He had tried spending less time with her, but that angered her, too, and made her accuse him of avoiding her. He had taken her to Italy, to the Lakes, to Scotland, even France—she met each with decreasing enthusiasm. He bought her jewellery that went unworn and books that remained unread. He tried to delve into the root of the problem with her, to speak openly of their sorrows, but doing so had had an opposite effect of the one intended. Nothing he had tried had ever improved her spirits, and by now, he was out of ideas.

The worst part of it was that she made him doubt himself. He was sliding back into his old, comfortable hauteur because it was easier than the constant wrong-footedness he felt. He was always stepping too hard, or speaking too loudly or too softly. Everything he did seemed to injure her in some way, and he could not bear to see the pained expression on her face when he did.

It was far easier to simply turn away.

The decline of a marriage rarely happened as a result of some singular catastrophe, Elizabeth found. Rather it was the day-by-day chafing, the little asides, the hidden insults, the small injuries, the seemingly inconsequential wounds that united to do so.

Elizabeth sat in the carriage across from her husband —across, because the days when he would move to sit beside her were long gone by now—unable to stop herself from studying him. It seemed almost incomprehensible that this cold stranger was the same man who had once stood before her in Charlotte's parlour and declared ardent love to her. She searched her mind, trying to remember his exact words that day, the tone he had used, the mode of his address, but she found she simply could not.

He looked up from his book. "What is it, dear?"

She blushed, embarrassed to be caught staring at him. "Um, nothing. Are you hungry? Lady Catherine's cook made us a nice basket."

She bent over and reached for the basket at her feet then pulled it into her lap to begin a search. "There are some delicious-looking pastries and salted beef, and some sugared fruits and—"

"It is nice to see your appetite returned," he said. "You ate so little while we were at Rosings, my aunt wondered if you were ill."

Resentment, always held just at bay, rose in an instant. "You and your aunt must consider that I am not as large a person as either of you," Elizabeth replied with carefully held serenity. "I simply do not eat as much."

"Even so, there were days I wondered if you ate anything at all, save a mouthful of soup or two."

"It would be nice if I could offer you a muffin without exposing myself to censure."

He closed his book and accepted the muffin. "You should not comprehend the loving concern of your relations as censure."

With such a tone as he used, Elizabeth wondered that frost did not form on the carriage seats. "I am merely astonished to find myself so fascinating that drawing room conversation must centre on me and how much I eat. Surely there must be something in the world of greater interest than that Elizabeth Darcy takes a muffin?"

"The fact that you do *not* take a muffin is more the issue." Darcy made a careful study of his own muffin, breaking off each piece and depositing it into his mouth with deliberate movements. He masticated pensively, turning his head towards the window. When he had disposed of three such bites in like manner, he said, in a low tone, "Having lost my family as I have, is it any wonder that I worry?"

"Georgiana did not starve to death," she replied immediately. "And neither shall I."

Lady Champneads, née Miss Georgiana Darcy, had died a woman's honourable death in the birthing chamber. The baby had died, and Georgiana had endured a dreadful, lingering death, occasioned by blood loss and fever that took her away over the course of three days. They were three of the darkest days Elizabeth could have ever imagined. She sat in an upstairs parlour at Henlow, watching her husband pace with impotent and suppressed rage before he eventually accepted his sister's death with hollow-eyed stoicism. It had been above two years since her passing, but Elizabeth still knew not if Darcy would ever truly recover from the experience, dreadful as it was.

Pity softened her. She reached for him across the divide, her hand landing on his knee. "The food at Rosings does not always agree with me."

"No, nor I," he agreed at once, offering a half smile. "Lady Catherine is far too fond of rich sauces."

They locked gazes for a moment, and Elizabeth could only suppose that he saw some invitation in her look. Half arising, he moved across the carriage, took a seat next to her, and unfortunately stepped directly, and hard, onto her foot. Unable to stop herself, she cried out. In a trice, he was back where he began, muttering apologies.

"No, no. It hardly signifies," Elizabeth protested. "It was an accident, nothing more."

She reached down to rub her foot, which pulsed with pain within the confines of her boot. "Pray, join me."

"No, no." He had picked up his book again. "I despise this carriage. It is too small and crowded. We cannot be comfortable in it."

Stung, Elizabeth released her foot and sat back into the plush squabs with a thud. This carriage was the one he had commissioned for her, shortly after their engagement. She still recalled the utter shock and delight she had felt on the day he presented it to her; she had never before imagined herself with her own carriage.

Like Darcy, she had supposed that one day this carriage would be replaced with a larger one, some roomy landau suited for a growing family—but that need had not arisen, and so they continued on with this smaller one. Perhaps she despised it, too, symbol of her failures that it was.

The remainder of the journey was passed in the tense silence that was, too often, the common mode.

CHAPTER TWO

GONE & PAST HELP

Darcy and Elizabeth arrived at the house in London with just enough time to dress for dinner. Darcy felt that he moved very slowly and heavily as he followed Elizabeth up the stairs to their bedchamber, his gaze fixed rather indecently on the movement of her bottom as she climbed upward, but his mind remained in Kent.

His man was finished with him at last, and Darcy left his dressing room, finding his wife staring blankly into her looking glass. "Are you ready? Shall we go down?" he asked her.

"Oh!" She startled. "I did not hear you. Yes, I am ready."

She rose and took his arm and they moved towards

the door. As they entered the hall, she said, "Does not this all seem rather silly at times?"

"Silly? What is silly?"

"Just that you and I, we have spent this time preparing ourselves, changing our clothes and going about this ridiculous ceremony... and for what? We might have just saved ourselves the bother and had dinner in our bedchamber. We could have sat on the floor in our dressing gowns if we so wished it."

Sat on the floor in a dressing gown? "Is that what you would prefer?"

"No—I am just saying we *could* have done, that's all." She gave him a smile. "A carpet picnic. They can be rather charming, you know."

He smiled back. "I daresay they can. I imagine you and your sisters must have had many such delights as girls?"

Her smile slipped, and he knew at once that he had erred.

She said nothing, but her lips had tightened into something that was not quite a frown. Her silence continued as they entered the dining room, and he assisted her into her chair.

He took his own chair, and soup was served to them. He was hungry—he scarcely even realised how very hungry he was until the first waft of savoury goodness hit his nose—and began eating at once. His bowl was nearly empty when he saw Elizabeth was doing little more than playing with her soup.

"Why are you not eating?"

She shrugged, not looking at him. "I rarely have an

appetite after travel. All that bouncing around in the carriage unsettles me."

"We need to rid ourselves of that carriage," he said immediately. "Perhaps a larger one, heavier, would be less likely to..."

His words died as Elizabeth looked at him, an unmistakable flash of anger in her eyes. She gave him a wordless, defiant look that seemed to dare him to continue. He dared not. He looked down and took another large mouthful of soup. "In any case, I am sorry you are unwell."

She said nothing, and he lapsed into his own thoughts.

It had not always been this way between them— indeed, far from it. He did not often allow himself to slip into memories of the past, fearing their sweetness would make his present situation too difficult to bear. However, today he would indulge himself a brief sojourn into the delights of his mind, the recollections of days of rosier hues. He considered several favoured remembrances, finally settling on one from the earliest months of marriage. April 1813—just after Easter, when they had been married for about four months.

Elizabeth had invited Lady Catherine and Anne to Pemberley, unable to tolerate the notion of being the cause of an estrangement in the family. He cared less about it than she did, but she was determined to heal the breach. Alas, when his relations had been there a week, he had been required to go to Derby, for some business or another.

She accompanied him to the carriage, her hand tucked into his, to bid him farewell. As his men loaded his trunks, she leant into him, murmuring, "Is there anything I can do to prevail upon you to return home tonight?"

"There is indeed," he said. "But alas, it cannot be done in front of our servants."

Elizabeth laughed loudly, pressing her hand to her mouth, but she had not acted quickly enough to avoid Lady Catherine's notice. Lady Catherine scowled at them and made expressive looks towards Mrs Reynolds and Chapman, who stood at a respectful distance, overseeing the bustle.

Darcy straightened and spoke in a calm, masterful tone. "Madam, you may be sure I will do all things within my power to return tonight."

Elizabeth did likewise, adopting her very best Mistress-of-Pemberley attitude. "I thank you, sir," she replied, her voice solemn but her eyes twinkling. "I should be well pleased to see you returned tonight but urge you to keep your safety and health at the foremost of your concerns."

He gently touched his hand to hers, whispering, "If I must ride through the darkened woods fending off high-waymen with a stick, so shall I do to return to my fair maiden."

"I will leave my lamp burning for you," she said.

She gave him one last smile as he climbed into his carriage. He presumed that she would have entered the house immediately—for it was still early spring, and the wind still had a bite to it at times—but she did not. Lady Catherine could soon be heard over the impatient snorting and stamping of the horses who longed to be off.

"Are we going to stare after the carriage all day?" Lady Catherine asked peevishly. "He is only gone to Derby, after all.

What he could possibly want there, I cannot imagine, but then again, who can comprehend the vagaries of man?"

Then after a short pause, he heard his aunt say, her voice half-incredulous and half-soothing, "Well, there, there now, it is not like he is off to war! Such tears are highly unseemly for a woman of your station!"

He left for Derby that day grinning broadly, imagining his lovely wife and the homecoming he might receive on his return.

Darcy tugged himself from April 1813, returning to his present, where his bride sat across from him, now breaking a roll into shreds and no doubt desiring his absence above everything. "What's gone and what's past help should be past grief." He had scarcely thought the words before they emerged, but it was too late to stop himself.

She raised her eyes from the bread she was destroying and asked, "What did you say?"

"Nothing," he said. "I was merely lost in thought."

"You said something about being past help?"

"A quote," he said. "Shakespeare, *The Winter's Tale*."

"And that's where your thoughts are? Quoting Shakespeare?"

He had no wish to begin arguing with her and so said, simply, "Yes."

She sighed unhappily, clearly suspicious of him but perhaps, like him, not wishing to begin a full-blown row. She had finished tearing the roll into bits and again picked up her spoon, using it to stir her soup about.

"I was thinking of that time... I had business in Derby," he began. "Right after we were married—Lady Catherine had come to Pemberley."

She stared at him uncomprehendingly.

"I was just remembering how... how reluctant you were to see me go."

"I am always sorry when business takes you from home," she replied, but her tone held little sincerity or warmth. It made him feel worse than if she said nothing at all.

"Are you?" he asked before he could stop himself.

She flashed a glance at him, and in the instant before she schooled herself, he saw a bit of her old fire. "Of course I am."

He decided he would go no further with that line of enquiry. Instead, he asked, "What were you thinking of? If I may be so bold as to enquire."

"Me?" She gave a half smile followed by a little grimace. "I was thinking of the time I danced with Mr Collins at Netherfield Park. You must recall it—that first autumn when Bingley leased it."

"The first time I danced with you," he said, noting that he sounded markedly wistful. "Yes, I remember it well."

"Mr Collins was always out of step," she said. "Always stepping on someone, always apologising, always making a bigger hash of things. There was just something clownish about him; he never quite got it right."

"That is quite true," said Darcy with a chuckle. "Is it my injury of your foot which has inspired these reflections?"

Elizabeth did not laugh in reply. "It's strange," she mused, "how things just get out of time that way.

Missteps and stamping on toes, and somehow you just cannot get things synchronic again."

Clearly, she was no longer speaking of Mr Collins.

"I cannot deny the truth in that," he said. Then, more boldly, he added, "It is too reminiscent of us, is it not?"

"Us? What do you mean?"

"We are constantly out of step, and I cannot determine how to right us, though I wish that I could."

His uncommon candour hurt her; he could see it in the way she turned her head, quickly and awkwardly, so that he would not see the tears which had sprung to her eyes. He saw them regardless.

"Has it come time for us to be frank?" she asked lightly.

"I always welcome your honesty," he said. "We have never been less than honest with one another, and I would certainly not wish it otherwise now."

"Very well," she said. Then, in a shaky voice, she asked, "I wonder sometimes if you wish I had died... that time. You would be finished mourning and could have remarried by now."

"I could never be finished mourning you," he said and reached across the table, intending to take her hand.

Either she did not see or did not choose to see. Her head remained turned away, her eyes trained on some point opposite him. "You must think of that, though. You could have had all you wished for."

In the past, he would have met such a statement with the reassurance that she was all he ever wished for. But they were well past such platitudes by now. He would not insult her by saying something that, frankly, was not true for either of them. There was more, a great deal more, that they both wanted, and it was not likely they would ever have any of it.

"I will not deny," he said, "that our situation grieves me. But what is there to be done?"

"I know we cannot continue on in this manner, but I hardly know what to do for a remedy."

"Nor do I."

He watched as she drew a deep breath, an air of steely determination coming over her. She met his gaze squarely and said, in a rush, "You will come to me tonight. I think if we can just—"

"Elizabeth," he said. "No."

"No? Do not tell me no, Fitzwilliam. Come to my bed, and we shall—"

"I cannot. Please do not ask this of me."

"But you must! If you do not, then what hope is there?"

"There is no hope at all and every possible risk," he retorted.

It was too unkind. She choked visibly on whatever words she had been about to utter then stopped a moment, getting her breath while he permitted himself to feel, in fullness, his regret. He had not meant to speak so, and naturally he had no desire to reject his own wife; it was the determined look she had on her countenance that had done it. She did not want *him*; she wanted to be about her business.

A pause ensued whilst each of them allowed themselves to recover from the monstrous honesty which had just been unleashed into the room. At last, tentatively, he said, "Forgive me—"

"For what?" She laughed bitterly. "You spoke from the heart, as I bid you do."

"I am simply tired of hoping and wishing and praying for something that will clearly never come to pass."

Her head bowed, she sat in silence for a moment before offering, feebly, "'Never' is a difficult word to comprehend at the present. I am only five-and-twenty, and—"

"We are both still young, and yet we are older now than when we began," he replied. "Surely our age, advancing as it is, will not afford any advantage over the lack of success in our earlier days, and with your health as it is..."

"My health? What is wrong with my health?"

He did not reply to her. She knew, as well as he did, that she had grown thin and pale and listless. Enough painful truth had been spoken already, and there was no need for him to add that. Gently, he said, "I meant in regards to your illness... before."

She rested her cheek on one hand. "Yes, of course."

She looked so sad, so bereft, it was difficult to bear. Now it was his turn to toy with his dinner, trying as best he could to escape the sorrow in her fine eyes. At last, he could bear it no more.

"I must go to Pemberley," he said abruptly. "Check on the... plantings and such... I shall leave... um... day after tomorrow, or so."

He did not invite her to come with him. Nor did she ask. She gave a small nod then returned to the task of introducing small sips of soup into her mouth. When she cleared that course in favour of heartier fare, she excused herself, her direction unclear.

He remained where he was, silent for a time, his eyes not straying from his plate. Then he took up his fork, calmly and methodically chewing his way through his dinner then sitting alone with a glass of port for the customary length of time. He then retired to the drawing room, unsurprised that he was alone therein. James, the senior footman, informed him that Mrs Darcy had retired.

He sent James to retrieve a book from the library for him and then sat, staring at its pages until he was sure Elizabeth must be asleep.

It would be one thing if he disliked her, but he did not. Indeed, he loved her as much now as he ever had, perhaps even more. The difficulty of her, he knew, was not her fault. She was as beset by sorrow as any woman ever had been, and that pain had changed her, as it had changed him too.

CHAPTER THREE

IN VAIN HAVE I STRUGGLED

Darcy always left with the dawn. Elizabeth, hearing him move about in his dressing room, rose and went to kiss him and bid him a good journey. He kissed her and wished her to keep well until he returned, and dutifully she urged him to hurry back. Then she returned to bed.

When she rose, later, she first took herself to her desk, whereupon lay all the letters of invitation which had arrived. She shuffled through them, seeing an endless array of parties she did not wish to attend and people she had no wish to see. But she would go. One thing she had grown accustomed to of late was being in town on her own. Saye and Lillian often escorted her about, but Lilly was approaching her confinement, so they would not likely stir. Briefly she considered asking one of her sisters to come to her but discarded the notion almost immediately; she had no stomach for idle shopping and silly conversation.

The park, she decided, would be her destination. Some time to reflect, to scheme and to decide.

About half an hour later, she set forth, suitably attired. She walked briskly and energetically, at least until she arrived at the park and was required to adopt more elegant strides. She went a distance and then found a bench. Sitting, she dug into her reticule, removed a book, and opened it, having no intention to read and every plan to watch her fellow park-goers.

Genteel poverty, she had learnt, announced itself in quiet ways: worn gloves and remade bonnets, a complexion that hinted at too many meals of potatoes and watery soup, and certain discomfited tension when matters of money or fortune were discussed. Elizabeth saw all these signs and more in Mrs Emily Clark.

She had not known immediately the lady's name was Emily Clark, of course. She had first seen Mrs Clark in Hyde Park in March, observing her as she sat in her dyed black gown, watching wistfully as some children ran about, expending their energies among the denuded trees and matted grass. Spring was just beginning to make its presence known in London back then, but the winter had been long for the little souls whose governesses and nurses tried valiantly to keep up with them.

Like Elizabeth, Mrs Clark was dark haired and dark eyed. She had a more impressive bosom than Elizabeth did, but Elizabeth believed she might be taller. Or so she thought, but then Mrs Clark stood to leave, and Elizabeth thought, *perhaps not.*

She had seen her more frequently as the weather grew warmer, and from this Elizabeth deduced a love of nature and the outdoors in the lady. The third or fourth time she saw her, the lady's friend arrived, calling out, "How do you do, Mrs Clark?"—and then Elizabeth knew her name. Mrs Clark's friend was genteel and had some money, as evidenced by the large carriage which lingered by the road, awaiting her. The two ladies spoke for a little while, and then her friend left. Mrs Clark turned her head, watching her friend disappear into luxury and warmth with an almost palpable yearning.

She wondered about her often. She had a kindly air about her, and every circumstance hinted at some recent tragedy. Elizabeth thought she seemed about the same age as she was, but from the absence of a ring or a cap, Elizabeth guessed she was not married; neither did she have her own child among the little ones who frisked and capered about. A widow? Possibly, given the black muslins.

It was a stroke of luck—or Fate—when Elizabeth met Mrs Clark's friend, the one seen in the park, at her own friend's soiree just before they went into Kent at the end of March. Mrs Adams was vivacious, pretty, and younger than Elizabeth at only four-and-twenty. Elizabeth sat with her among a group of ladies for a time before she could say, in the most natural accents, "Oh! I daresay I have seen you before!"

"Have you?" Mrs Adams put her teacup down on the table between them, seeming eager to know when Elizabeth had seen her.

With feigned diffidence, Elizabeth apologised. "I happened to be on a bench nearby when you were speaking with your friend in Hyde Park one day—Mrs Clark, I believe? I see her there often."

"I am sure you do." In a confiding tone, she added, "Dreadful business, poor dear. She has not had it easy."

"No?" Elizabeth asked politely. "I am sorry to hear it."

"Husband died by the same fever that took their wee one."

"Oh, that *is* a dreadful business," Elizabeth said, with true sympathy.

"And," said Mrs Adams, "left with absolutely nothing but a pile of bills and a pretty smile, for however much good any of *those* will do her. She will be out of mourning in June, and I said, 'My dear! You simply must remarry! There is nothing else for it.' But she cannot think of it. Quite in love with Mr Clark—I never myself saw much in him, and a better man would not have left her in such a way. But she believed he hung the moon." Mrs Adams shrugged. "If not, she shall have to seek a position. Companion to a wealthy lady, perhaps."

"She is gently bred?" Elizabeth asked.

"Oh yes," Mrs Adams assured her. "Her father's estate was in Shropshire, but her cousin inherited now. She cannot go to him to be sure."

"Ah." Elizabeth hid the wince that accompanied this notion. How much like Mrs Clark's her own situation could have been!

Mrs Adams was pulled away then, forced to speak to someone on the other side of her; by the time she turned back, it might have seemed awkward or officious to ask more about Mrs Clark. In any case, Elizabeth had heard enough. Mrs Clark—the name would go on her list.

Now, some six weeks later, Mrs Clark was still in the park, and still in her dark-hued gowns, mourning her husband and child. But she did smile. Elizabeth had to admire her for that.

In the end, Elizabeth spent the days of Darcy's absence idly. She ignored a good proportion of her letters, she declined nearly all invitations, she walked at unfashionable times and in unpopular places to avoid people she had no wish to see, and she took her meals on a tray. She did read—quite a number of books, in fact. But that was the whole of it.

It could not last, of course. Eventually, Jane called, and, being very familiar with the ways of the house and the mistress, would not be turned away. Mrs Hobbs came into Elizabeth's dressing room with the news. "Mrs Bingley has informed me that she knows you are here and does not intend to go away until she sees you."

Elizabeth smiled faintly. "You tried telling her I was away?"

"Her cook saw you walking yesterday morning," Mrs Hobbs reported.

"Ah." With a sigh, Elizabeth said, "I guess I shall see her then."

A few moments were required for Elizabeth to make herself more presentable; a nicer gown was donned, her hair was pinned up a little tidier, and she had her maid put the faintest hint of colour on her cheeks. Jane was forever fretting about Elizabeth's pallor.

When she entered her drawing room, Jane rose immediately, coming to her with a face that was all smiles. "Lizzy!" She kissed Elizabeth on both cheeks and then hugged her tightly. The two sisters then settled in to one of Elizabeth's favourite sofas—a rose-hued velvet situated perfectly by the window—for some nice sisterly chat. Jane had a litany of concerns over her children. Though she had not inherited Mrs Bennet's tendency to fret over her own health, she did like to look for trouble in every sniffle or tremor in her two babies, Stephen and Sophie. Elizabeth kept one ear on the conversation—making all the appropriate soothing noises where needed—while the other examined Jane.

Jane was presently with child, the third time in less than five years of marriage. Her succession of pregnancies had left her soft and round; even her pretty face had taken on the appearance of bread dough slowly rising in its bowl. Her rings cut grooves into her fingers, and she grew winded from the exertion of climbing into a carriage—but she was happy.

With a little shake of her head, Elizabeth mentally scolded herself for such uncharitable thoughts against her most beloved sister. Jane was still beautiful, and Bingley was as besotted with her as ever, so what did it really matter? Her own trim figure was surely nothing to be pleased with when one considered what it signified.

"Is that a new necklace?" Jane asked, gesturing towards her sister's neck, where a thick, double strand of exceptional quality pearls rested.

Elizabeth smiled indulgently as she leant over to

allow Jane her examination. No one loved jewels like her sister did. "They are exquisite," Jane breathed, reaching out one plump hand.

"Darcy gave them to me a few days ago. Not really the thing for morning calls, I know, but what is the use of being married to a wealthy man if you cannot not make your own rules once in a while?" Elizabeth forced a little chuckle.

"A few days ago?" Jane leaned towards Elizabeth, her face kindly in a way Elizabeth knew meant trouble. "Why?"

Elizabeth's heart skipped a little, but outwardly she remained calm. "Just because. He does that, as you know."

"Yes, of course." Jane leaned back and studied her sister pensively. "I believed he had gone to Pemberley."

"He did." Elizabeth rose from her seat and went to the window, peering out at a blue sky. "They were on my dressing table yesterday morning. I suppose he left them with my maid before he went to Derbyshire."

"He did not give them to you directly?"

"No." Elizabeth could feel Jane's eyes boring into her back. Her sister used silence in that way, forcing confessions from her; it had worked for years, but Elizabeth was determined to resist.

"Perhaps they are an apology?" Jane prodded gently.

Elizabeth shrugged, still looking out the window. She could not deny it, not wholly. "Maybe," she said vaguely.

Fortunately, Mrs Hobbs entered the drawing room just then, bearing a tray laden with delicacies, and Elizabeth went back to the chair opposite her sister. Cook's specialty was a lemon-cheese tart and held the centre of the tray, which also included fruit and more coffee. Elizabeth felt her throat clench and her stomach roll at the sight of it all; the sugary decadence felt revolting to her, but Jane's eyes lit the moment she saw it.

"You must be starved." Elizabeth put on the smile she thought of as her 'entertaining-the-*ton*' smile and pointed at the table, indicating to Mrs Hobbs where to set the tray. The housekeeper did as bid and served Jane a large piece of the tart, then quietly departed.

When the door closed behind her, Jane said, "Caroline told me that she saw Darcy near his club on Monday." She took a bite of the tart and then added, "Two days ago."

"Yes, I know when Monday was," Elizabeth said with deceptive mildness. "Why does your sister-in-law concern herself with the whereabouts of my husband? She ought to be worried about hers. I hear he stays at Almack's playing cards until all hours of the morning."

"Never mind Caroline." Jane reached out to lay her hand on her sister's. "Why is Darcy staying at his club?"

"Pray do not plague me with your sister's gossip because I do not care what she thinks she saw—"

"Lizzy, sweetest. Please tell me what's wrong. Perhaps I can help in some way."

With that, her silly protestations stopped. Elizabeth felt herself cracking under the strain of Jane's solicitude. She had no wish to share with anyone the dreadful business of her marriage to Darcy, but the silence had grown too heavy. Her hand shook and trembled under Jane's, and Jane curled her fingers around it.

"I did not know he was there," she admitted in a small voice. "But it does not wholly surprise me."

"No?"

"We... things are not well."

Jane stayed silent but gently rubbed her hand.

"He..." Elizabeth began, but her voice cracked, and tears began to spill. "I am a failure, and I despise myself for it, and he resents me because of it."

"That cannot be. He loves you, and you know that."

"Oh, Jane." Elizabeth sighed and shook her head. "I came to this marriage with nothing, as you well know. In matters of fortune, I was a loss to him. In the matter of connexions and family, I was a degradation. But I always assumed that giving him children would redeem me. A country girl! We all know the jokes; no doubt he expected at least three or four by now."

"You and Darcy want only for a bit more time, and I am sure—"

"More time?" Elizabeth laughed bitterly, swiping away her tears. "Jane, we have been married as long as you and Bingley have—nearly five years! You have two children and another on the way!"

Jane sighed, her pretty face creased into worried lines. "Even those who are barren—"

"I am not barren," Elizabeth interrupted her sharply. "Not wholly, in any case. I was pregnant once that I am sure of. Perhaps there were others that were too early for me to truly know."

"You miscarried?"

Elizabeth nodded then rose, suddenly unable to bear being idle. Fortunately, her sewing basket was nearby. She retrieved it then began to rifle through it while she spoke.

"The first and second years of our marriage were...

disappointing, to say the least. I admit I was worried about it, fearing that I could not give him the heir he needed. At one time, I spoke to a midwife in Derbyshire to see what could be done for the situation, and she gave me some sort of elixir to drink to help me. It made me dreadfully ill, but I kept at it. She told me it would pass, once I grew accustomed to it."

"Did it?"

"Not really," said Elizabeth. "Though soon enough I hardly minded how awful it was because it seemed to work. Almost immediately my courses ceased, and my bosom—well, it has never been anything to boast of, but it was changed. My maid and I both saw it."

"And then?"

"And then I returned to the midwife, and she said... she said it was not to be."

"What?" Jane exclaimed. "But the signs—"

"It can happen," Elizabeth replied with a little sigh. "Evidently, sometimes, when you want it so badly, your body plays a trick on you. A dreadful, cruel trick."

"Well, I simply do not see how," Jane declared, reaching for another piece of the tart. "If you mean to tell me that mere wishful thinking can make a woman's bosom grow, why then I—"

"But, as you see, there is no child," Elizabeth said patiently. "So clearly, she was right. After that, we decided to give up for a time. Georgiana was engaged by then, and we had plenty to do with seeing to her marriage."

Elizabeth found the needlework she wished for and began stabbing and poking the fine muslin beneath her fingertips. "Then, more than a year ago... the Festive

Season it was... I lost a child that was... well, it all seemed very certain. Until it was not."

She had to stop here. Though over a year had passed already, it still affected her deeply to recall the sense of shame and failure and the agony of seeing the disappointment in Darcy's eyes.

"The pain was... it was..." Elizabeth inhaled deeply, willing the film of tears which had covered her eyes to dissipate. "Bad. Very bad. However, the worst of it all came later, when I became ill. Fever, chills... They said my body had failed to rid itself of everything, and at one point they told my husband he must call my family and arrange my funeral."

"Oh, Lizzy." Jane gasped. "But none of us knew! Why did he not tell us?"

"I was delirious with fever, so I cannot answer that question. Darcy chose to take it on himself. He was yet mourning his sister's death, so to see his wife enduring something of like nearly sent him mad. I was too ill to protest, too ill to really even care, if you must know the truth.

"But he was wonderful to me, utterly devoted to my care. I did not realise it immediately, of course, because I was so very ill, but he would not heed the words of our doctor. He was vigilant, right by my bedside, nursing me through it all. I am, as always, persuaded that it was his love for me which saved my life, which brought me back from the brink of oblivion."

"He loves you a great deal. But I do wish I had known. I would have helped you!"

"You have your own babies to concern yourself with," Elizabeth told her. "You are needed at home. In any case, he saved me. My recovery was long, but I am perfectly well, although the doctor thinks it unlikely I should ever conceive again."

"Lizzy." Tears welled up in Jane's eyes as she reached for her sister. "Lizzy, pray do not listen to them. These doctors are all charlatans—"

"We have had every opinion there is to have," she said. "Some say I cannot conceive. Others say I can but will not carry the child. Darcy thinks if I could only get past my anxiety... but is there anything more anxiety-provoking than someone telling you not to be anxious? In any case, it hardly signifies."

Her needlework had been forgotten. Elizabeth rose, allowing it to fall onto the floor. She needed to walk, to put some distance between her words and her heart. "My marriage has... It has unravelled. He pays me all the attention that duty requires of him—I can complain about nothing—but there is no affection, no passion, nothing between us like it once was. He never comes to my bed anymore, and he stays elsewhere at times, though I try to keep his home as agreeable as I can. Some days I have greater success than others, to be sure."

She sank into the closest chair. "Of course, by now, after months, years of this cold existence, things have become more difficult. An argument is always at the ready for us both, making conversation difficult, if not impossible. We both, I believe, look for shades of meaning even if there might not be any. I feel I misunderstand him constantly, and I am sure he feels likewise. He has again become the man I met at the Meryton assembly years ago—reticent, disgusted, and, oftentimes rather unlikeable."

"And you believe it all stems from your difficulties in childbearing?"

"Jane, you cannot imagine the strain that being unable to have children places on a marriage." Elizabeth sighed. "We simply cannot get past it."

"Perhaps if you talk to someone else—"

Elizabeth waved her off, watching with fascination as Jane made her way through another slice of the tart. "We have spoken to apothecaries, midwives, physicians... We have tried all of their suggestions, and it has led to nothing."

Jane sighed and then very carefully asked, "Do you think he has taken a mistress?"

A mistress. Elizabeth nearly laughed aloud at the thought.

"No, I do not, and I pray I am not the sort of wife who is blind and stupid to it, but... I see no signs of it. As you have said, he is at his club, not sidling out from the mews behind some unknown residence."

"So what can you do?"

Elizabeth thoughts had moved to her plan, the nascent ideas which had twisted about in her brain since Kent. She looked at her sister and, for a moment, considered confiding in her. But no, this was so far beyond Jane's understanding, she could never condone it. Like everyone else, she believed that if Elizabeth could only be easy about it, to stop fretting and dedicate her energies to loving her husband, success would be the work of a moment.

"Whatever came of that governess you were speaking to? Miss Lloyd, I believe her name was?"

Jane blinked, no doubt surprised by the turn in the conversation. "Oh... well, she had not the character we thought she had. In any case, the children are still too young, of course."

"Her character?" Elizabeth picked up her tea and sipped it.

Jane leant forward, not a gossip but often eager to share some news. "Miss Lloyd is, as it turns out, not actually a Lloyd."

"What do you mean?"

With a prim countenance, Jane said, "Her family have cast her off. She... was engaged, and it appears that she anticipated her vows and fell with child."

"Indeed?" Elizabeth took another measured sip. "Well, that is as much a reflection on his character as hers. Where is he now? Where is the child?"

"He abandoned her, and the child is being raised by a relation. But the tale was known abroad, and it would not erase the stain. Such a shame, too, for she was terribly clever and kind. In some ways, she reminded me of you."

Elizabeth nodded. "I saw her once, and the resemblance was quite startling, save for her eyes. Blue, I believe?"

Jane wrinkled her brow and considered a moment. "Maybe. I do not know if I really looked. I am surprised you did, though, Lizzy. Why are you so interested in Miss Lloyd?"

Elizabeth did not reply.

CHAPTER FOUR

HIS ABHORRENCE

May 1817

Elizabeth could never forget the sacrifice that Darcy had made for her, back in 1812, before they were married, back when he knew not if his efforts would ever yield him his heart's desire. He had contrived to assist a man he loathed—a man who had so injured dear Georgiana—and see him settled with her sister. Lydia, the silliest and most imprudent of all her sisters, had courted scandal and had been rewarded accordingly. However, she and Elizabeth and indeed all of the Bennets were saved from absolute ruination by Darcy. So far did he go that he actually served as witness to Mr and Mrs Wickham's marriage, had signed his name to vouchsafe for them, provided them their living —he had seen to it all.

She still remembered how it felt to comprehend what he had done. To know that he had done it for her, that he loved her still—it had been heady and humbling and heart-warming all at once.

Now was the time for her to return the favour. Could she do for him that which made her very heart revolt against her? Could she act contrary to all she felt if it would bring them peace? What if this could be her gift to him? She would still give him a child, only in an unusual way.

She twisted and turned it over, examined it from every side over the course of the two days until he returned. It sickened her and filled her with fear; but she could see no other solution.

She did her best to smile and be friendly when he returned, behaving for all the world as if she thought he had been at Pemberley and had only just returned. "And how did you find things in Derbyshire?" she asked cheerfully, taking hearty bites of beef. She had ordered a very sturdy menu that night and wanted to eat enthusiastically before him.

"Everything was as expected," he said; and that was that. Privately Elizabeth wondered if he had ever even gone to Derbyshire, but it did not matter now. She rattled on while he ate, reminding herself to eat until she felt her stomach swollen against the bottom of her stays.

"It is good to see you in such spirits," he said when dinner was finished. "It seems that it has been too long since I have seen you thus."

"Yes, well..." Elizabeth swallowed. "I have done a great deal of thinking while you were gone."

"Have you?"

Their butler, Danforth, entered with Darcy's port then, and Elizabeth fell silent, waiting while he poured her husband his drink. Her heartbeat began to crescendo wildly as she watched Danforth pour with what seemed to be excessive deliberation, but at last it was done.

"Danforth, will you see that we are not disturbed?" Elizabeth asked. If the butler was surprised, he did not show it. He merely nodded and quit the room, closing the door behind him with a firm thud and click.

Her request had raised Darcy's concern, and he regarded her with a furrowed brow. "Do you wish to speak to me of something particular?"

"I do." Her mouth suddenly dry, she swallowed. "So... next week I will be six-and-twenty. It is... I confess it feels like something of a difficult age. Youth is behind me, and yet I feel just the same as I ever did."

He smiled blandly. "You are in every way just as youthful and beautiful as you were the day I met you."

"The day you met me, you said I was not handsome enough to tempt you," she reminded him. "But never mind that. My point is that everyone else my age is married, many of them with children, and those who are not have resigned themselves to spinsterhood."

His smile slipped into trepidation. This subject never ended well for them. He took a careful sip of his port while he arranged his thoughts. "Elizabeth, we have a happy marriage and a beautiful home. We have not been blessed with children, it is true, but I believe in due time—"

"In due time? If it has not happened now, it is not likely, and in any case—" She paused a moment and cleared her throat. "In any case, I do not see much chance of a conception whilst my husband refuses to come to my bed."

Darcy went pale, and he set his glass onto the table with exceeding care. He looked at her steadily, and his tone was grave and excessively reasonable when he at last spoke. "The doctors said you should not conceive another child. He believed that—"

"No, the doctors said I *could* not. That is quite different from *should* not, and in any case, no one is in agreement. One doctor tells us this, and this midwife says that, and it's all a jumble."

"It is not a risk I am willing to take," he said firmly.

"And is yours the only opinion worthy of consideration?"

"You have no idea what it was like," he retorted. "How near death you came. I would much rather live without children than live without you."

"You do live without me!" Elizabeth cried out and then immediately hushed to a tone less loud, though still impassioned. "Our marriage is coming apart. You do not share my bed, you kiss me only if I ask you to, we scarcely speak to one another, we do not laugh together... You just went to Pemberley and did not even me ask if I wished to accompany you."

She paused and then, looking at him straight on, asked, "Unless, of course, you did not even go to Derbyshire?"

His eyes flashed towards her, dangerously dark. "I beg your pardon?"

"Perhaps you were in London the entire time."

"Do not be ridiculous."

"Perhaps you should tell Caroline Slaghorne not to be ridiculous when she is telling everyone she saw you at Brook's when I thought you in Derbyshire." Elizabeth paused and added more softly, "She and all the rest of the gossips have seen that something is amiss between us and very much enjoy discussing it amongst themselves."

His eyes had gone nearly black. He stared at the table linens as if they held some solution to this tangle. "I did, in fact, go to Derbyshire, but yes, I returned earlier than planned."

"And stayed at your club?"

He nodded, not meeting her eye.

"Why did you not come home?" She cursed herself for asking a question she did not wish to know the answer to and for asking it in such a plaintive way.

He ran one hand over his mouth. "Because I hate this too."

Though he said nothing that Elizabeth did not also feel, it stung deeply. They sat in silence, considering it. "There is an ever-widening breach between us. We need something to bridge that if there is any hope of us finding one another again."

"I will try harder," he said by rote. "Perhaps, once the—"

"No." Elizabeth stopped him immediately. "That is not what I mean. We are in need of something far beyond the usual measures by now. We cannot leave this room with nothing but vague promises of walks and talks to remedy things."

Finally, he looked at her. He reached for her hand, and she slid it into his grasp, feeling comfort in the warm familiarity of his touch. He sighed. "I want you to know that I would do anything to set us back on course."

"I would too," she said, imbuing as much meaning as she could into the words. "Absolutely anything at all."

"If only there was something we could do that we have not already tried," Darcy said regretfully.

"If we had a child, or hope of one," Elizabeth began slowly, "I would no longer feel like the mistake you made."

"I have never thought of you as a mistake. Not once."

"No?" she asked quickly. "You cannot tell me you do not have some regret. With each and every crestfallen look I see on your countenance, my disappointment in myself increases accordingly."

"I am not disappointed in you," he said, with such earnestness that she nearly believed him.

"Well, you should be," she replied softly. "It is my chief duty, as the wife of a great man, to produce his heir, and in that I have failed. I have disappointed myself, and I should think you a simpleton if you thought otherwise."

He made no reply to that but squeezed her hand reassuringly.

"If there was a child, you would no longer look disappointed, and I could live without the never-ending strain for giving you a child. We would not have the fears of Pemberley going to your cousins." With a deep breath, she said, "I have grown up watching what happened in a marriage that was marked by my mother's inability to give my father an heir. I do not want that for us."

"It would never happen that way for us."

"It already is," Elizabeth insisted. "You have slipped back into disdaining me, and I feel it."

He let go of her hand and ran his own hand over his face. "What could we do that we have not already done? You have taken the waters of nearly every health spa England has to offer. We have consulted midwives and physicians, bishops and clever women—I know not what else we might do."

"I have a suggestion." Elizabeth's heartbeat sounded like thunder in her ears. This was it; once she said it, there was no going back. "But it will require some... some discomfort on the part of us both."

"Oh?" His brow wrinkled. "What is it?"

Elizabeth drew one final, shaking breath before saying, "Your mistress could have our child."

"My what?" He shot out of his chair so quickly the chair fell backwards with a crash. He nearly shouted, "Is this another of Mrs Slaghorne's rumours? I will not stand for this. I shall go right over there—"

A footman opened the door to see to what was happening, but Elizabeth waved him away. "Pray sit down."

A sense of calm came over her, strangely coupled with the feeling of a heedless tumble down into she knew not what. She was surrendering to the inevitable, and her terror had been swallowed into serenity. "No one has accused you of having a mistress—not to me, anyway."

"You cannot think I keep a woman!"

"No, I do not." On his look, she said, more vehemently, "I assure you I do *not* think you keep anyone." Rising from her chair, she attempted to soothe him, running her hand up his arm. "I have never suspected that, even once."

"Then how can you suggest—"

"Sit down," she urged him. She helped him pick up the chair, and then he helped her sit again and took a seat himself. He was only marginally calmer; his face was flushed, and a vein throbbed in his temple.

"I do not accuse you of having a mistress—not now in any case. What I mean is that you could take one and with her, conceive our child."

"I would never so dishonour you or myself," he snapped.

"Will you please just hear what I have to say?"

He sat with his jaw clenched and his head turned away. "You cannot think this of me. I should far prefer you again accuse me of ungentlemanly behaviour than to say such things as these."

"I have turned this situation around in my mind for months now, and I am certain you have too. There must be a child, and there is no other way to get one."

"Illegitimate children cannot inherit an estate."

"The child *would* be yours and would be therefore legitimate."

"And what of the effect of this on our marriage?" He sent her a fierce glare. "How will that do, when I present to you my son, born of an illicit tryst?"

"First of all," she said, "the child would be my own, as much as if my womb had carried it. No one would ever know that he was born of anyone but me. Secondly..."

She swallowed, hard. "I cannot deny that the thought of you with another woman pains me beyond anything I could ever imagine. I have conceived this notion in utter desperation. We are foundering, you and I, and drastic measures must be taken. I am willing to put aside my fear for this, for us, if you will too. It is a sacrifice for us both, and I do know it. I could never tolerate it if I did not think that it might just save us."

He softened as she spoke, his hard, angry countenance becoming sympathetic and sad as he really looked at her for the first time in months. His expression gave her the courage she needed to continue, to tell him of her plan.

"This is what I propose," she began. "We shall undertake a journey to the Continent—Vienna, Rome, Germany, wherever your fancy might direct us—after putting about our intention to see some noted physician who has novel methods to aid childless couples. We will tell our family and our friends and naturally beg secrecy so as to ensure as many find out as possible."

He did not smile at this little attempt at a witticism.

"For this journey, I would engage a companion," Elizabeth continued. "A lady of gentle breeding, someone who looks like me—a governess or an impoverished widow, perhaps."

"Except instead of being there for the purpose of your companionship..."

"She would be there to... to become pregnant with your child." Saying it did not get easier with more utterances thereof. "She would be your mistress until a child was... was sure."

"And then what? You have this companion who is with child and—"

"And we would stay, wherever we were, until the baby was born."

"No." Darcy shook his head. "No, no, no. This is absolutely the most ridiculous, most abhorrent thing I have ever... What if she did not have a child? Then what? All this for naught, and we are right back as we are!"

Elizabeth replied, "We would place a limit to the amount of time we shall spend in this endeavour. Perhaps a year?"

"A year?" He stared incredulously. "You expect me to be having relations with some other woman for a year?"

"We would be certain the lady you chose—"

"I am not choosing anyone!"

Elizabeth sighed. "Very well. The lady *we* chose would have some history with pregnancy, so we knew she was able to conceive."

"It cannot be done... I cannot do it. There must be another way," he said. "Something... some method—"

"There is not. You know we have tried everything."

"The doctor told me that if you could only rest and keep your nerves—"

"There is nothing as likely to provoke anxiety as someone telling you not to be anxious."

"Elizabeth." He leant towards her. "You are asking me to go against everything I have been taught, every principle, every moral, every bit of reason."

"I know. I do not pretend your part in this is easy,

but neither is mine. We will both sacrifice a great deal in this plan," she admitted. "In truth, I am not surprised by your immediate disgust of the notion. But we need this. You and I need it. Pemberley needs it—it is not an easy sacrifice to be sure, and I would never say that your part is easier than mine. But if I can do it, then I daresay you can too."

Darcy slumped over the table and rested his forehead on one hand. He remained so for a long time before he abruptly sat up, stood, and exited the room.

CHAPTER FIVE

THE MOMENT FOR RESOLUTION

W here he went after that and during the next day, she knew not. She would not stoop to asking Fields, his valet, but she did not hear him in his room either that night or the next morning.

I must have some consolation that he does not have a mistress, she thought. *Else the prospect of getting one should not anger him so.*

Elizabeth had a book on her lap when he knocked on the door to her bedchamber later that night. It caught her by surprise, such that she dropped the book over the side of the bed then had to scramble from beneath her blankets to retrieve it. Because she was up, she went to the door and opened it, finding him standing there, in his nightshirt and dressing gown.

His countenance was inscrutable, but the smallest

finger on his left hand beat an irregular rhythm on his thigh: he was nervous. Warmth flooded her to think that after all of these years, and so much trouble, she could still make him nervous. He had been recently shaven.

Elizabeth leant against the door frame, resting her cheek against the cool wood. "I was worried about you."

"I... yes, forgive me. I should have left word."

"Where did you go?"

"Matlock House," he replied. "Saye was there, and it grew late, so I slept there."

A full day complete? she forbore to ask. "How are they?"

"Expectant," he replied.

It was a hard word to hear, and it made her lower her eyes. "Yes, I should imagine so."

She heard him heave a heavy sigh. "When I saw her, when I see how they are, I think to myself that I would do anything if it could be us."

"Yes," she said with quiet urgency. "So would I. *Anything.*"

"But what you have asked of me—I just... I cannot. It is contrary to every sense of duty and honour—"

"Even if it saved Pemberley? Saved us?"

"It would more likely destroy us," he said.

"Not having a child is destroying us." She raised her eyes and offered a faint smile. "Damned if we do and damned if we do not—but perhaps it is better to fight than to wither away?"

"Are those really our only choices?"

"What others do you see?" she asked swiftly. "Have we not tried all else?"

In her head, she willed him to please avoid saying

they wanted for time or that she should relax or any of the other useless platitudes that had been offered to her, to them, in abundance.

He reached towards her—easily, as they stood only inches apart from one another. He wound one of her curls around his finger. "I only want for us to be *us* again, for our house to have the felicity we once knew."

Me too, more than you know. "It is hard, so hard, to have any measure of joy knowing each and every day how I have failed. Do you not see that? The only thing I might have given you, to your family and to Pemberley—and I failed. I brought *nothing* to this marriage, not even a womb that adequately performs its office."

"Elizabeth, I never think of it in that way."

"I do, and every single day, it weighs upon me. I feel…" She swallowed, feeling her ever-present sadness rise within her. "I feel like an intruder in this life, like I have stolen something that should never have belonged to me."

He reached for her, pulling her into his arms, tight against his chest. She could hear the steady, reassuring thud of his heart. "My heart was made to belong to you," he murmured. "Never doubt it, for I do not."

"As mine was made for you." She ran her hands up his back, feeling his body temperature rise as tension, a different sort of tension than they had had of late, built in his body. "Always."

They stood there, their breathing somehow falling into unison, as it always did. *Does he want me to invite him in? Does he think an invitation is required?*

She whispered his name. "Do you want to—?"

His hands sank into her unbound tresses as his

mouth found hers; for long minutes they stood there, basking in the glow of reunited lovers. They moved then, Elizabeth walking backwards, until she felt the backs of her legs touch the bed; then they both climbed onto the mattress together. They lay for a moment, husband and wife, looking into one another's eyes.

"Will you tell me one thing?" she asked. When he nodded, she said, "Is this some last effort to try and—"

"This has nothing to do with a child," he said. "This is only for us." And then something in his eyes changed, and he rolled partway towards her, his hand reaching for the hem of her nightgown and pulling it up and over her head. She leant up, allowing him to remove the garment from her and drop it off the side of the bed. His own soon followed it, and all the while he whispered in her ear, "You are so beautiful, my dearest, loveliest Elizabeth, and you must allow me to tell you..."

With that, he proceeded to woo her with commingled words of lust and love, and Elizabeth counted it a very good step towards all that they needed so dearly.

Some time later, she laid in his arms in a way she had not since they were newly married. His mouth rested near her hairline, and he kissed her temple periodically as one hand absently stroked her hip. It struck her then how their most recent marital relations—which were, in fact, not very recent at all—had been so very different. The intimacies of marriage had become their chore; their marital bed a place of duty, not desire. Elizabeth felt a pang of guilt as she recalled the times she had wished he would simply hurry up and finish, or even—she shuddered to remember!—the times when all she had really wanted to do was read her book.

She regretted her part in allowing it to become thus. She was not so long married that she could not remember the fevered days of their courtship: the crisp autumn air kissing her legs that time that he dared to run his hand up her leg; the day they were kissing at Oakham Mount, and she had dropped his neckcloth in mud, and they had laughed while they attempted to make it presentable again; or, most wonderful of all, the day or so prior to their wedding when he had taught her not to fear but to delight in that which was to come.

Could she wonder that he had elected to remove to his dressing room? *He must think of these memories, too, and repine what had been lost. No, not lost,* Elizabeth told herself. *For we have managed to find it again, in some measure at least, even if temporarily.*

She felt his chest rise and fall against her back as he moved from sated lethargy into sleep. She wondered if they had reached an agreement.

Darcy woke in the night, the weight of Elizabeth on his arm having caused pins and needles to afflict him. He gently eased it from beneath her, careful not to dislodge her from his side, and then lay for a moment, thinking.

They had left the curtains open around their bed, which meant the faint glow of the fire illuminated her a little. She had her face, as was her custom, pressed into the pillow so he saw only her hair. He ran one hand over it, very lightly so as not to disturb her slumber. It was frightening at times, how much he loved her. He had always believed he would do anything for her, asked or unasked—but this? He could never have imagined such a request as this.

The very thought of lying with another woman nauseated him. In truth, he knew not if even he could physically manage it. And even if he could sire a child under such appalling circumstances, would he forever look at the child and remember them? And no matter what she said, he could not imagine that Elizabeth would ever look at him the same way. How could she, knowing he had dishonoured her and their wedding vows?

A Gordian knot if ever there was one. Darcy inhaled deeply, the scent of Elizabeth's hair drifting into his nose. Her own blend of the essences of pear and freesia —even now, the scent made his body tighten with the faint stirrings of longing.

He distracted himself by recollecting his conversation with Saye the night prior. He had met him at their club and then gone home with him; Lilly was spending a great deal of time in bed, and Saye was bored, never an ideal circumstance. When bored, Saye would either grow peevish or mischievous; to save them from either, Darcy offered to come back and play chess, offering various wagers on certain moves to further appeal to his cousin's interest.

They had dined on a meal fit for male appetites—beef and bread and ale—and then retired to his lordship's book room for their game. "See there," Saye mentioned as they were setting up the board. "Ink, right on the desk, soaked through the blotter. Three earls have sat at that desk and now..." He shook his head disgustedly.

"How did that happen?"

"How else?" Saye snorted. "Beelzebub."

Fitzwilliam's wife had given him a son in quick time following their wedding in the summer of '13. The boy was now age three and every bit as untamed and energetic as his father once was. "A pity that the military will not have them sooner," Saye said often. "Even the navy makes you wait until they are seven."

Fitzwilliam's son had been christened as Basil Bernard Fitzwilliam. Saye, within moments of the child's christening, had styled him Beelzebub, and nothing anyone could say would dissuade him from calling him thus. To make matters worse, the child had begun calling himself "Beez-buh," which Fitzwilliam insisted sounded was his way of saying Basil, but which everyone else knew was the child's attempt at Beelzebub.

"You must stop calling him that," Darcy said with a chuckle.

"We found him in here attempting to drink from the inkwell," Saye replied incredulously. "He has had two nursemaids quit in tears!"

"The first nursemaid had an offer of marriage," Darcy replied, his eyes scanning the chessboard. "And the other, a sick father who needed her care."

"The boy will be dead before he's breeched," Saye replied with dark surety. "Pray to God above that this protuberance of Lilly's proves to be male. Else I do not know what shall come of Matlock."

Matlock Hall and the fortunes associated with it were not entailed, Darcy knew, but the earldom was another matter entirely. The earldom was an ancient one, nearly three centuries old, and but for the stubbornness of their great-great-great grandfather, should have been a duchy. It occurred to Darcy, then, how Lilly's anxieties might have had something to do with their own delay.

"A great burden it must be on Lillian," he mentioned. "All those disappointed earls standing behind you, should she birth a girl."

"In truth, I hope the first is a girl. 'Twill inspire her to keep working on it." Saye chuckled at his own joke then added, more soberly, "I daresay I have Beelzebub to thank. Took the anxiety right off. The duty discharged, she could really enjoy the diversion of it all."

Recalling himself to his present, in his bed with his beloved by his side, Darcy pondered those words. *"The duty discharged..."*

Of course, he had no brother whose wife might obligingly 'discharge the duty,' nor did he have any possibility for a nephew on the Darcy side. That fell to Elizabeth. Else Pemberley would be in the hands of young Mr Cooper Darcy. Strangely, that prospect had begun to trouble Darcy less; it certainly paled in comparison to watching his marriage run aground.

Elizabeth rejected outright the notion that her nerves had anything at all to do with their predicament. "I am not my mother," she said often and with increasing indignation. "And in any case, if nerves should be the source of our tribulation, then tell me how my mother managed five children in seven years? For her nerves are as demanding as any I have ever known." He could neither argue nor refute the point.

She also insisted, many times, that the strain of wishing for a child had not even begun to leave its mark until two years had elapsed. He knew not if that was wholly true. Jane had fallen with child almost immediately after she and Bingley wed, and Darcy knew, even if Elizabeth would not admit it, that she could not long bear to be outdone by Jane.

Having drifted off in the midst of his musings, Darcy woke to find the bedchamber bright with sunlight and his wife gone. Only as far as the dressing room, he thought, hearing the low voices of Elizabeth and her maid, Dylan.

Some minutes later, she entered. "There is my Sleepy-Head," she chided sweetly.

"How late is it?"

"Almost ten," she said; and he saw then that she had clearly already been for a walk, dressed as she was with her hair slightly wind-tossed. She came and perched beside him and ran the backs of her fingers across his cheek. "I suppose you must have needed it badly. Have you not been sleeping well?"

She said it in the most light-hearted of accents, but her eyes were anxious, searching his, no doubt hoping for clues to his thoughts or temper. Reaching up, he said, "I have always found the sight of you, after a walk, particularly fetching."

As had been his hope, she blushed. So encouraged, he followed his sally by sitting up a little and pulling her into his arms. She came willingly, allowing herself to be pulled back into bed with him.

Some time later, they both sat down to breakfast. Not only had she some bread but also a cup of chocolate, and he considered that a very good sign. Only quite recently she had pronounced that chocolate made her gorge rise. He said nothing of it now but watched with quiet encouragement. Surely if she were not so frail, so often tired or nauseated…

"What if in the midst of it all, with such exertions and sacrifices—not to mention the possibility for a scandal—you were to fall with child yourself?"

She glanced up at him. "I have considered that. I think the possibility of that quite… quite slim, to be truthful."

"Slim but not impossible."

"No, not impossible—but likely so. I know what you think of me, but it is not mere anxiety at the root of this. Indeed, I am quite sure it cannot be."

"How?" he pressed.

"How?" The tenor of her voice changed; she was becoming frustrated with him. "A woman knows her body, that is all. Look at Jane; look at Lydia, or Kitty or Mary, who will likely only lie with her husband when she is positively required to do so!"

"Elizabeth—"

"Even the Collinses! Four children they have now, and Charlotte quite determined to keep her door closed henceforth. She has borne Longbourn's heir even before she was its mistress."

He reached out and grasped her hand. "I only question you because… because I want to know there is nothing to hope for before… before I can be a party to something so drastic."

Her fingers curled around his. "Fitzwilliam has told me, on the battlefield, of men whose legs turn green with infection," she said, more calmly.

"Why he thinks it sound to speak to a lady of such atrocities, I shall never know."

"Men tossing about with fever, who are knocking on death's door, and so they cut off the leg to save them—and it does."

"Sometimes it kills them," Darcy said.

"They are near death anyway… and sometimes it *saves* them. The latter happens oft enough to make it a valid practice."

"I just do not know how I could do it," he said; and it was wholly true. The very idea of it! Of going to another woman, of knowing her intimately as his wife—it was impossible in every way.

"Please?" Elizabeth's eyes glistened with her pleading. "I beg you to find it within yourself to do this, for me. I cannot abide the thought of it myself but surely for the greater good…?"

Darcy nodded, very slowly. At length, he rose from the table, bent over her, and kissed her head. "Pray allow me time to think of it?"

"Of course," she said, twisting her head to look at him. Hope shone naked in her eyes, but he could not yet be reconciled to this path, and so he only kissed her again and said, "Shall we go to the theatre tonight?"

"I would like that," she agreed.

CHAPTER SIX

WILLING TO HOPE
FOR THE BEST

June 1817

Anthony Goddard Fitzwilliam was born to Saye and Lillian early in June. Lillian, having two elder sisters, had plenty of ladies to attend her in her birthing chamber, so Elizabeth had not gone to join them. Instead, she and Darcy went together to meet the new heir of Matlock some days following.

Fitzwilliam met them in the vestibule of the Matlocks' town house. "Wait until you see him," he said with a laugh. "He is enormous and has a head like a billiards ball. How he did not manage to kill his mother, I shall never know."

"How is Lilly?" Elizabeth asked as the housekeeper helped her out of her pelisse.

"Very well indeed. She will be glad for your visit."

With a smile towards Darcy, Elizabeth left the gentlemen and headed towards Lady Saye's bedchamber. She had become familiar with the house long ago and knew just where she went. Darcy turned the opposite direction and went to his uncle's study to congratulate the new father.

"Did he say my son had a head like a billiards ball?" Saye demanded as soon as he saw them. "Because if he says it again, I assure you, I shall run him through directly. That is the next earl of Matlock he treats with such disrespect."

"You have styled my son Beelzebub," Fitzwilliam remarked genially. "Turnabout is fair play."

"Darling, do not fight your brother," Lady Matlock scolded from her chair. "All babies are bald."

"Except mine," Fitzwilliam said smugly. "Mine had a fine head of curls, very handsome."

Saye shot a murderous look at him. "Perhaps so and yet, he will still likely grow to look like you, as my son will grow to resemble me. Now tell me who shall emerge superior?"

Fitzwilliam laughed again. "You really need to let the boy go to the nursery. You are clearly not sleeping, and it is making you excessively ill-humoured."

Saye looked as though he might actually strike his brother, so Darcy hastened to change the direction of the discussion. "You do not let the boy go to the nursery? I confess you do look rather tired."

"He will go there eventually but not yet."

"Why ever not?"

Saye shrugged, playing with the lace at his wrists.

"Seems rather a hard thing, does it not? Poor thing was so comfortably ensconced, and now we are to send him off to fend for himself?"

"It is hardly fending for himself, Saye," Lady Matlock protested. "The nursery gets heat from the kitchens—if anything, it tends to be too warm in there. He shall do very well."

"For now, he likes to be with Lilly." With another defiant glare towards them all, he added, "And so do I."

The door opened then and a footman admitted Elizabeth who bore in her arms a small, tightly wrapped bundle, the nurse trailing behind her.

"What do you think of his head, Elizabeth?" Saye demanded before even getting to a chair.

"It is as fine a head as any I have ever seen," Elizabeth replied staunchly. "Ideally suited for a young earl-to-be."

"See there!" Saye said to the room in general. "Just so. Elizabeth gets it."

Elizabeth brought him to Darcy and held him in a manner that would display him. In truth, his head was rather large and rounded, but then Saye had also had a rather round head in his boyhood. Darcy hoped Fitzwilliam would forbear to tell his brother so.

Darcy held him a moment, examining him. It always amazed him to see a baby and be able to recognise the people in the family who had preceded him. Young Anthony had very much the look of Lord Matlock save for something around his eyes that was very much his mother's. He had no doubt that the Goddards would see their family traits more clearly than he did.

What would it be, he wondered, to see his own

65

father or mother reproduced in his child? Would it be a source of distress—and how great would be that distress —if Elizabeth could not see anything of the Bennets or Gardiners in her child?

Likely far less upsetting than if the child never existed at all.

Darcy handed Saye's baby back to his wife, who took him to a chair by the window and by his grandmama. Lady Matlock drew close immediately, murmuring and adjusting his blanket and smiling and cooing at him.

There were no tender meetings of his gaze and his wife's—gestures of that sort had ended long ago. But as Darcy sat, talking to Saye and Fitzwilliam and listening to them tease one another, he watched his wife. Elizabeth had a sweet curve to her lips and naked, fierce hunger in her eyes. He wondered if Lady Matlock observed it too.

Some time before they left to return to their home, Darcy knew that he had reached a decision. It was true they were not the first couple to suffer this problem, but neither would they be the first couple to resort to an extraordinary and uncommon solution. *Extremis malis, extrema remedia,* he told himself. It would be done—and done for the best.

The next days passed in equal parts sweetness and agony. Sweetness because, for whatever cause, they seemed to be once again in accord. They were once again dancing in step with one another, following the patterns in a way that had both familiarity and the thrill of newness. The thick dark clouds of woe had cleared, at least for now, and she enjoyed basking in the sunshine with him.

But it was agony to be unknowing of his thoughts. She supposed she ought to be glad he had not rejected the scheme outright—well, in some sense he had, but now he was thinking about it. She could ask for no more, she reckoned.

When it had been nearly five days complete, Darcy came to her as she sat at the small escritoire in her study, reading the various notes and letters which had come in, inviting them to dine here or dance there. He had some pages in his hand and kept hold of them as he began pulling a heavy, flowered armchair towards her.

"Shall I summon James to do that for you?" she asked.

"No," he said. "I should like to speak privately to you."

"Very well." With as much patience as she could muster, she waited for him to sit. When at last he did, he studied her for a moment before saying, "It has long been my wish to go to Naples and spend some time among the ruins."

A thrill tore through her, but she knew not if it was time for exultation. "Naples? I daresay that would be very agreeable."

"I have been to an agent," he said. "Making the enquiries for arrangements for myself and my wife and... and m-my wife's... companion."

The breath she did not know she had been holding released in a gasp, and tears rose to her eyes. She closed her eyes for a moment, terror and felicity and joy threatening to overwhelm her.

Darcy continued to speak as if by rote, his voice flatly authoritative. "We should go rather soon. In the event we must cross the Alps, one must be over by September. But perhaps we shall go to Nice and cross over the Gulf of Genoa into Rome. In any case, we shall move quickly until we reach Rome and then spend more time on the northernmost sights on our return. I would very much like to see Lake Como."

A vision leapt into her mind, herself standing next to him on the shores of that magnificent lake with their son swaddled in her arms. Her arms ached, sometimes, wanting a small bundle held within them. To envision it within reach, even in theory, was exhilarating. She could see it, a small face with dark curls, who would look up at her every day knowing she was his or her mama—it took her breath away, imagining it, imagining it to be within her grasp. Yes, she could do this. She could share her husband if it meant that precious bundle would become a reality. She would do anything at all to have that child.

"I would like that too," she said, choking a little on the words.

He then passed to her the pages from his hand. Elizabeth took them and began to read. Her eyes widened momentarily when she saw with what thoroughness he had undertaken to make an arrangement between them and this as yet unknown woman who would do so much for them. The sum he had offered was more than generous, and she was glad for it. After all, they would purchase not only her womb but her silence. She wondered what the lady would do with it afterwards.

Would she remain on the Continent? Or come back to England?

"You have thought of everything," she said softly. "Every angle, every detail."

"Not everything," he said. And then, with a faintly sick look on his countenance, he added, "Not... her. I cannot... I am not going to have a part in the selection of... her."

"None at all?"

"I will not take a mistress," he said, with sudden fierceness. "That is not what this is. This... lady, she shall provide for us some... help. But it is not for me. I do not care if she is tall or short or dark-haired or has missing teeth."

"I understand," Elizabeth said. A brief silence followed until she said, "So you will wish me to choose her, then?"

One short jerk of his head was all the assent she should have, it seemed. But it did not signify; she was ready. She had done some preliminary work in finding suitable candidates for this.

He said nothing as she described them to him. All three of them resembled her in the most basic of ways, and all were gently bred ladies who had fallen on some misfortune or another. Mrs Clark she had met in the park, and Miss Lloyd had applied to be Jane's governess. The third was a lady called Miss Harrington who Elizabeth had only just learnt of. That lady's father had recently died, leaving her with nothing. She had a terrible stepmother who wished her out of the house, but she had not yet found herself with any likely position. Elizabeth liked her less than the other two because she had not proved her capacity to bear children as yet, much though she might have enjoyed helping the girl.

Darcy rose half-way through her recitation, went to the window, and stared out. He said nothing at the conclusion of her recitation.

After a few minutes of silence, she ventured, "I-is there one that seems better than the others to you?"

His voice sounded strange when he replied—a little hoarse and certainly fraught. "You decide."

Elizabeth waited another moment before saying, "Very well. I shall."

He turned on his heel then and quit the room, leaving Elizabeth to her hollow triumph. And a hollow triumph it was for having so long centred her energies on gaining his agreement. Now that she had it, other feelings would intrude.

Mrs Clark, Miss Lloyd, Miss Harrington. She reviewed them in her mind, wondering should she choose the prettiest or the least pretty? The cleverest? The stupidest? The sweetest? What qualities should prevail when one chose a mistress for one's husband?

A mental image came then, Darcy and the unknown, as-yet faceless woman, somewhere in a bed together. Nausea rose beside a panicked scream that threatened to overcome her, and she bent, arms wrapped over her stomach to prevent it.

Stop that! She was sharp with herself, forcing herself to replace the vile imagining with the better one: her, the baby, Lake Como. That image would be the only one she could permit in her mind, the baby and nothing else. All others would be pushed aside.

CHAPTER SEVEN

A VERY GENTEEL,
PRETTY KIND OF GIRL

The drawing room at Abingdon House was crowded and hot, and Darcy disliked it violently. It was the fashionable crowd, mostly people enamoured of their own importance, and one could not pull a decent conversation out of anyone.

That is to say I cannot. He looked over to where his wife stood laughing and smiling among a little cluster of ladies and a few gentlemen too. *She seems to have no trouble with it.* He considered going to her, but in this group, to hang about one's wife was considered unseemly and dull. He could generally count on Saye at such parties, but Saye was with Lilly and his son, as he should have been. The evening promised to be exceedingly long; dinners at Abingdon generally lasted above three hours, and once the obligatory time of port and cigars was tacked on... Darcy rubbed his temples discreetly and moved towards a group of men he had been at school with.

Half an hour later he was by the window, hoping to see a driving snowstorm that would send them all scurrying home. Unlikely, as it was June, but a man could dare to dream. He was thus when a cool feminine hand slid into his. "Darling, I am afraid you are not enjoying yourself," Elizabeth murmured beside him.

"Do not distress yourself for me." He turned, looking down at her. She looked beautiful, he thought; her cheeks were pink, and her eyes sparkled in a way he had not seen in some time.

It astonished him—perhaps more than it should have —to see how the shackles of grief and worry and failure had fallen from his wife once they had made up their minds. She became again, the teasing, witty girl he had fallen in love with, and he felt himself easing back towards being the man worthy of that girl. They became truly freed, remade into the lovers they had once been before miseries of obligation and duty overcame them. They spent more of their days together, shopping, walking through the park, and reading together in the library, and he had loathed the need to go into society and give up a night of sweeter pursuits. Lady Abingdon was not, however, one to be rejected.

She looked up at him, her lips pursed, then said, in a voice even quieter than her previous murmur, "You are considering how *in*supportable it would be to pass many evenings in this manner." She said it in the manner that Caroline Bingley once had, in that lady's overly affected manner—Darcy had told her that tale once, of the long-ago conversation at Lucas Lodge where he had admitted to the first flush of his admiration of her.

"While that might be true," he teased in reply, "for now I am meditating, once more, on the pleasures of fine eyes in the face of a pretty woman."

She laughed, and in a gesture hidden from the room, he offered her arm a little caress. "You cannot regret this party. You are quite the favourite of nearly everyone here, it seems."

She inclined her head. "Perhaps not as much now, as I have been forced to tell several of the ladies I shall not be available to help with their assorted causes this year. They are very curious about our journey and more than a little envious of us."

If only they knew, he thought.

"What say you to running off?" she asked.

They had been speaking of their journey, so he first misunderstood her. "We are going to run off."

She laughed lightly. "I meant now." She looked around at the pressing horde of exalted personages and whispered, "Let's go home."

He lowered his head to hers. "They will never be able to detangle our carriage in time."

"We can walk. They can bring it back later."

He laughed. Was she serious? It was she who had insisted it was necessary to come tonight and she who had spent a great deal of time at her toilette getting ready for it.

"It cannot be half a mile," she added.

"We cannot just run off," he said.

"We can if I feel a dreadful headache coming on." She gave him a mischievous smile then took his hand and began to tug him away from the window. "Truly, I can hardly see straight. Such is the agony."

He followed her, delighted but uncertain. This had been something of an issue for them once; he needed no one but her, but she liked to be out and about and make friends and attend parties. "Elizabeth, do not do this on my account," he said. "I shall be perfectly content, I promise you."

She was ahead of him now and gave him an appealing glance over her shoulder, a shoulder that happened to be draped charmingly with one long curl. "I do not think I can live with perfectly content, sir. I must see what I can do to send you into raptures."

Some hours later, he lay beside her in her bed, reflecting that she had indeed done just that. They had made their excuses to Lady Abingdon, who exclaimed her dismay over the evils of headaches. Elizabeth had promised she would call before they departed for the Continent, and then they had very nearly raced back to Darcy House, relying on a footman to tell the coachmen to bring home their carriage when possible.

Times like these, when their marriage seemed renewed, made him sure they—and he—had done the right thing. It was not all perfect, of course. Real problems had risen between them, but like weeds in the garden, they required plucking out. But at last, they were doing that, resolving problems, understanding each other, and making progress towards healing their marriage and making sure those vexations and griefs would not plague them again.

Reaching down, he moved a lock of hair away from her face. It would work. It had to.

One fine Thursday morning in early July, Darcy returned from a ride in Hyde Park. He entered the house to be met by Fields, who told him, with excessive gravity, that Mrs Darcy wished him to meet her friend in the drawing room.

Darcy, in the act of tugging off his gloves, said absently, "Who is it?"

"A Mrs Clark, sir. Mrs Darcy did not say why she wished you to particularly meet her."

And suddenly Darcy understood. Careful to keep his emotion from Fields, he said, "By all means, then."

Fields helped him change his clothes and neaten his appearance in a far too short time; too soon, Darcy found himself feeling like men who approached the scaffold must, resolutely descending the stair and going towards the parlour where Elizabeth sat with a woman she believed should become his lover. *No! Not a lover, not by any stretch!*

When he entered, he found them sitting side by side on the sofa. Mrs Clark was a pretty woman who looked rather like Elizabeth herself, and yet she repulsed him on sight. For not the first time he lamented the dreadful state of women, whereby circumstances beyond their control required them to fall on selling their own bodies to survive.

"Mr Darcy," said Elizabeth with a hopeful, searching smile, "this is my new friend Mrs Clark."

Mrs Clark rose and curtseyed very nicely. Elizabeth invited him to sit opposite them. Darcy did, wishing for all the world that this terrible interview would be already concluded. She wore widow's weeds, he observed. He made that his opening for conversation. Gesturing towards her skirts, he said, "My condolences. It seems you have suffered a recent loss."

"It will be a year complete on Tuesday next," she said. For a brief moment, her mouth tugged downward into a frown. "He and my son fell to a dreadful fever that ran through our village."

"I am sorry to hear it."

Elizabeth quickly eased them all into a discussion that was as comfortable as it could be, never mentioning the truth of what bound them there until at last she said, with a look at him, "Mrs Clark has never been to Italy."

Most unfortunately, his eyes happened to lock with Mrs Clark's at that very moment; Mrs Clark blushed as she said, "It is a true privilege to imagine having such an opportunity now. I believed I was destined to become a washerwoman or the like."

Think of that, Darcy counselled himself. *A miserable fate awaits this woman; but for a few months' service, she will be nicely situated to remain in genteel comfort for her entire life long.*

He inhaled deeply to shore up his determination then said, "You will enjoy it, I think. The climate alone is…" And with that he rattled away, speaking of it as if there were nothing untoward about any of it, as if they were, all of them, intending nothing more salacious but to go on holiday together.

When the meeting was at last concluded, several matters had been resolved. They would sail in late

August, the payment was more than generous, and Elizabeth would see to it that Mrs Clark had all that she needed to travel comfortably. From the pink of her cheeks and the delight in her eyes, Darcy could see his wife was thoroughly suffused with happy wishes and expectations, and he mentally affixed the image of her as she was in his mind for the more difficult times to come.

In some ways he had to marvel—how had she come to accept this, the notion of him with another woman? It had to be nothing less than an almost lunatic desperation for a child.

Some hours after Mrs Clark left, Elizabeth invited her husband to walk with her. It was not yet the fashionable hour which suited her purpose; she hoped they might talk without interruption or the need for pretence. *Ah, for the solitude of Derbyshire! There we might shout if we wished, and no one would be the wiser.*

Darcy had seemed unsettled since Mrs Clark's visit, and she could not be surprised by that. Who could not be, faced with such as they faced? But Elizabeth thought that candour and honesty would serve them best through this and was determined to begin it now.

She held his arm fast and stayed close to his side as they walked, waiting until they were some distance in before enquiring, "Did you like her?"

She felt the slightest of stiffening in his bearing. "She seemed a very kindly, genteel sort of lady."

"In a certain light—or at some distance—one might mistake her for me."

He did not reply.

"But more so than her appearance, it is her character which draws me to her. She has a warmth and a wit about her I like very well. Even in so short an acquaintance, I can tell she has an innate good humour."

Darcy stared straight ahead as he said, "All admirable qualities, to be sure."

"I like knowing that, while she will be a great help to us, so too will we help her. I cannot think how she might support herself, much less attract a husband in such penury."

Darcy did not reply for some long moments. At last, he said, "It is a shame, how some men do not take seriously the obligation to their widows. These are unpleasant considerations, to be sure, but necessary."

Elizabeth waited for him to say more, but he stayed silent. At length, she said, "There were some other ladies to consider and—"

"Elizabeth." He glanced down at her. "If you find Mrs Clark suitable, then let it be done. And for all that is holy, pray let us stop talking about it."

"Very well." Elizabeth fell silent, understanding her husband's need to avoid saying more than was absolutely necessary on this subject. But his disposition did raise in her the oddest of notions—what if Darcy did not desire the mistress she chose for him? Was there some possibility he would not be able to... to... But no. She dared not rest her mind on such notions even briefly. He would do as needed done. She trusted him in that, with her whole heart.

On the evening before they left, Jane and Bingley hosted a small dinner to bid them farewell. Lilly could not be there, of course, but Saye was, and Fitzwilliam with his wife, Sarah. The Hursts were there; they had suffered their own delays—which Elizabeth privately attributed to Mr Hurst's affection for drink above that of his wife—but had then produced two pretty little daughters. One always knew a Hurst child because they did not dress as children; the girls, ages four and three, always appeared to be about to attend their coming-out balls. Should Caroline ever have a child, Elizabeth did not doubt it would be the same for her daughter.

Her sister approached her in the drawing room before they dined. "What I cannot comprehend," her sister complained in a low voice, "is why Italy of all places. What can an Italian physician know that a good London physician does not?"

Elizabeth smiled at her. "We do not know, either, which is why we are going to see."

"And do you really think it needful to remain there so long?"

Elizabeth inhaled patiently and said, "Should I fall with child, I must remain under the good doctor's care until the end." In a lower voice, she added, "Knowing what we have endured as you do, you cannot doubt that I will do whatever is needed if it will work."

"Of course," Jane owned, chastened. "But I do hope that this Mrs Clark will be of use to you—if you cannot have your mother and sisters nearby, you will need her help!"

If only you knew the sort of use she will be to me. Reaching over, Elizabeth took her sister's hand, saying lightly, "I wish I might have you by my side, but I do not think Bingley would be willing to part with you for that long."

Both ladies looked over to where Bingley and Darcy stood with Saye by the window. Saye was telling them some story which induced chuckles among the other two. Elizabeth smiled beholding her husband; she had always thought him handsomest on those rare occasions when he was overtly and enthusiastically mirthful.

"I will miss you desperately every moment I am gone," she told her sister. "More than you can know."

Jane had also noticed Darcy's more relaxed demeanour. "I daresay this scheme of yours has offered you hope, and for that I am grateful. But Lizzy, you must write to me faithfully and tell me all!"

To this, Elizabeth only smiled and kissed her sister's cheek.

CHAPTER EIGHT

NO SMALL DEGREE OF SURPRISE

The small party set out early on an August morning, Darcy having arranged all the travel particulars for them. He had decided that the largest part of the stay in Italy should be in Rome, the accommodation in Naples being less to his liking. "We shall go to Naples for a week or so, later," was all he said on the matter. Elizabeth was pleased to hear it; they had been in Rome shortly after their marriage, and she found it comfortable. Comfort was paramount; she knew well this was no sight-seeing excursion, so feeling at home was likely best.

In the interest of arriving in Rome more quickly, they had chosen to travel to Italy via Nice then sail to Rome. In Nice, they stayed at a lovely hôtel which overlooked the sand and the sea; after mere moments of contemplating it, Elizabeth decided she must go for a long walk to truly admire it.

Additional considerations made her wish to absent herself from the hôtel; she had urged her husband to be about his business. She hoped he would heed her, but it did not follow that she wished to be present for it.

She had broached the subject with great hesitation the evening prior. Darcy had continued to come to her bed, and inasmuch as she enjoyed the renewed closeness between them, there was a task to be accomplished. What was right to be done could not be done too soon, she always believed.

She made an attempt to treat the subject light-heart-edly but could not vouch for any success with that. Darcy, once he comprehended what she spoke of, had grown embarrassed and slightly vexed and accused, "Did you not tell me to act with utmost discretion? Surely you do not want to know...?"

"Of course not," she said hastily. "Only I... I wish to be sure something is happening?"

A long pause had ensued, after which he said, "Be assured that I am acting in the best interests of our marriage and our family. You have nothing to reproach me for."

"Thank you," she said immediately. "I know you will do as is best to be done."

Of course she also knew that Mrs Clark had had her courses of late, but they had ended the day prior. So it stood to reason that today...

She had walked out onto the *Camin deis Anglés*, but she did not see that. Instead she saw, in her mind's eye, them, together, in Mrs Clark's bedchamber, coverlets askew and...

Did they talk and laugh together? Or was it all business? Did he find Mrs Clark more appealing than she? She had grown too thin, she knew that, and her bosom was reduced to almost nothing. Did he dislike her sharp angles compared to Mrs Clark's softness?

Stop, stop, stop, she scolded herself. Her mouth was filled with a sour taste, and for a moment she thought it was coming—that she might vomit right here on the promenade. She paused a moment and closed her eyes, summoning again to her mind that image which always delighted her: herself on the shores of Lake Como with the small dark-haired bundle in her arms. She could never quite fix a face on the child, but she could feel the warmth of it in her arms, that peculiar blessed weight. She envisioned Darcy behind her, looking over her shoulder at the precious countenance and the feeling of completion she might have at last.

"Madame?" A man and woman stood near her, evidently alarmed by some strange Englishwoman who was standing in the middle of the path with her eyes closed. She shot them an embarrassed smile and then hurried off.

Strangely, the nausea would not subside. Elizabeth woke the next morning, her husband next to her, to the same metallic taste in her mouth, the same discomfort in her stomach. Actually boarding the ship could only make it worse and strangely it seemed to grow, day by day.

It was an excellent distraction from her ill-timed bouts of jealous imaginings. She instead fixed on her own nausea. She tried everything advised to her by the stewards and midshipmen, ginger tea and fixing her gaze on the horizon and sleeping on the floor, to no avail. Mrs Clark was a dear to her throughout, nearly running herself off her feet attending her and bringing her plain salt bread to nibble on.

It was something of a surprise—though perhaps it should not have been—to find in Mrs Clark a dear friend. The two ladies had much in common, from their interests to the similarities in their minds, and conversation flowed easily between them. It became easy to forget Mrs Clark's true purpose; most days Elizabeth fancied it really was like she was there simply for Elizabeth's companionship.

Darcy had begun uncomfortable and silent—even a little haughty—when he was around Mrs Clark. But they were not gone three days before he seemed to relax a little. He spoke more often and with greater ease, and he even laughed a few times. There were times she despised it; times when he was absent and she wondered, her gut twisting, where he was, what he was doing. There were days she wished to scream at him, which was absurd because he did no more than what she had commissioned him to do. She swallowed them all down, always taking solace in the image of the baby which would rest in her arms.

In Rome, Darcy had found for their party the most ideal of all possible accommodations: two adjacent apartments which were part of a former English gentleman's palazzo. It was exceedingly comfortable and pleasingly decorated, and it afforded them all their privacy. The Darcys' rooms were bright and airy, and Elizabeth felt immediately at home. The palazzo had, already, a large retinue of well-trained servants who were available to their needs, and they soon found themselves very happily situated.

On her first morning in Rome, Elizabeth woke in a film of sticky, sour sweat, her gut boiling. She sighed, willing it to pass from her. She had presumed to imagine that it would, once the rolling of the seas and the bouncing and jostling of the carriages had ceased, but it seemed her stomach needed some time to comprehend that it was over for now.

"I began to think you would sleep all day." Darcy arrived in their bedchamber, bringing the warmth of the sunshine outdoors with him. He looked flushed and exercised, and an immediate pang hit Elizabeth—had he been with Mrs Clark? Why did he look so... so relaxed? She sighed at her own silliness, forcing herself to appear good-humoured.

"I find myself exhausted," she told him with a smile. "But you must have been at it early." She winced when she heard the phrase 'at it', but he did not seem to notice.

"Fear not," he assured her. "I have only been walking about the piazza. I knew you could not like it if I saw the sights without you. The characters in the market alone shall require days of your study."

He said this with an indulgent grin after which he added, "Shall I ring for the maid?"

Elizabeth found herself overcome by a peculiar and uncharacteristic sensation—languor. She knew she ought to wish for it. Ordinarily, she should want to fling herself into the day headlong and immerse herself in the Italians and Rome and all the lovely, wonderful things beyond her window.

She was simply too tired; the idea held appeal in theory but not in reality. The very notion of removing from her bed, of dressing—even of eating!—seemed an impossibility.

"Do you think..." she began hesitantly. "That is to say, I am still quite fatigued from our travels. I daresay I could use a day being a lazybones, if the notion of that does not distress you dreadfully. I promise I shall be restored tomorrow and eager to see any and all sights you wish."

"Of course." He came to her bedside and bent over her, kissing her forehead lightly. "Do not concern yourself, my love. I shall shift for myself today."

But her languor persisted over the next few days, as did her seasickness. She found herself explaining the malady to her maid Ana Santina as she dressed her one morning. As Ana Santina did her hair, Elizabeth yawned so much that the maid had to scold her, using words that Elizabeth did not wholly understand, though her tone made their meaning clear.

Her hair suitably arranged, Elizabeth rose from her dressing table... only to find herself gripping the edge of it as saliva flooded her mouth, and a cold, clammy sweat broke out over her skin. She closed her eyes a moment, willing the dreaded nausea to recede, but it would not do. "I-I... I m-must..."

She sank back into the stool while Ana Santina, alarmed, ran to retrieve a cool cloth for her face. Elizabeth, eyes closed, felt the cloth's welcoming sensation tracing across her face several times, but though it was soothing, the nausea was unrelenting.

At length it did relent, just a little bit, and Elizabeth rose from the table on shaky legs. The sickness was still there but in the background now. She favoured Ana Santina with a weak smile.

"*Perdonami*. I fear I have not yet lost my seasickness from our travels."

Ana Santina gave her a doubtful look. "*Il mal di mare?*"

"It was a difficult passage." In truth, it had not been, but Elizabeth could think of no other explanation. "The sickness has plagued me quite dreadfully indeed, the worst I have ever known it."

Thick black brows covered Ana Santina's eyes, the colour of which reminded Elizabeth of a chestnut mare Mr Bennet had once kept. Those brows knit together in undisguised scepticism, and the maid cast Elizabeth several suspicious looks as she went about tidying the room.

Italian was not Elizabeth's best language, but in an effort to make Ana Santina comprehend the source of her troubles, she did as best she could, explaining how the illness had begun with the rolling of the sea and the jostling of the carriage as they came. Her words must have persuaded Ana Santina that Elizabeth had greater facility with the language than she did, for Ana Santina paused in her duties and began to rattle away, speaking quickly and gesturing with great enthusiasm. She spoke too quickly for Elizabeth to understand her, save for one word which leapt from the rest and struck Elizabeth forcibly—*bambino*.

"*Bambino?*" Elizabeth laughed. "No, no."

She smiled a knowing smile and shook her finger at her as she continued straightening the things on her table. "*Il mal di mare? No, no! Bambino!*"

Her words made Elizabeth stop short. She again clutched the edge of the dressing table, although for a much different reason than before. *Bambino?* Baby? No, surely not. She sank back onto the little seat and stared at her own countenance in the looking glass.

Ana Santina quit the room still chuckling and clucking at her as Elizabeth stared in the mirror, immobile with shock. It was in every way impossible... was it not? No, no, no, no, no, no, no. If Darcy knew... if it was true... could it be true? Elizabeth did some rapid mental calculations. Her courses... Well, yes, her courses were late, quite late, in fact, but since the time of her most dreadful miscarriage, the time she had nearly died, her courses were infrequent and irregular. It meant nothing at all.

Further, when she had been with child before, that all-too-brief time, she had not been so terribly ill. She had experienced a few days of some queasy feeling but nothing a piece of bread would not conquer. Any reasonable examination of such facts concluded that her present malady was seasickness or traveling sickness or whatever anyone wished to call it, but it had nothing to do with a child.

In fact, she had to conclude that she must ardently hope it was not a child. If it was, it must surely lead to another miscarriage, one she might not survive. Thinking of that made her think of Darcy.

He cannot know of this—he cannot even suspect *it.* Darcy had his marching orders, and this would be only a distraction and a distress—if indeed it was anything, which it most likely was not.

"No," Elizabeth whispered to her reflection in the looking glass. "It is nothing."

CHAPTER NINE

DISGUISE OF A
CERTAIN SORT

She lay in the bed before him, wretched and pale, sweat
soaking the linens around her. He had, in turns, stoked the fire
to produce near-intolerable heat and thrown wide the windows,
allowing in the cold winter wind. Neither had seemed to help.
Elizabeth would die.

Her respirations had become death rales. With shaking
hands, he ran a cloth over her face, doing anything he could to
make her more comfortable in this, her deathbed, never ceasing
in his prayers to God to allow him just one more day with her,
his beloved.

The sensation of the cloth roused her, and her eyes flew open
to stare into his gaze, angry and hard. "You did this to me,"
she hissed. "This is all your fault."

With a ferocious jerk, Darcy pulled himself into wakefulness and away from the hated dream. Elizabeth lay beside him in their bed, peaceful and cool, her face bathed in silvery moonlight from the window and her breathing measured and sedate. He gently brushed the backs of two fingers down the side of her cheek and then removed himself from the bed to go stand by the window.

Unlike many young men of his station, Darcy was not an enthusiastic gambler. His father had told him sternly that he must never wager more than he was willing to lose, and in truth, he was never willing to lose much. Yet, here he was, having laid a life-or-death wager in the riskiest and most important gamble of his life. Would he win? Or would he lose it all?

When Elizabeth had come to him with this mad notion of him lying with another woman, he had been infuriated, hurt, and incredulous; it had been Saye who had twisted it about for him, reminding him that it was the birth of Fitzwilliam's son which had enabled Lilly to relax and conceive their own son. "Let her think you are tupping some other woman," Saye had opined. "She is an unusual sort, that wife of yours, but I daresay she is not intending on joining you in the bedchamber to see to it that you perform admirably."

"I cannot deceive her, Saye," Darcy had retorted. "I shall not. Disguise of every sort—"

"Do not be a blasted fool with that 'disguise of every sort' claptrap. All of us need to hide little hurts from the ones we love sometimes."

That was Saye for you. A self-absorbed rattle who at times tossed off the greatest insights of all.

From there, Darcy had written to the physician in Derbyshire who had attended Elizabeth during the miscarriage. The man's opinion at the time was that she neither could, nor would conceive again. But if she did, Darcy asked him, would there be reason to suppose that another miscarriage would result? Could there be a repeat of the near-death illness of before?

The man's reply had been an unwavering no. No, he did not think Mrs Darcy showed any indication that she was unable to carry a child, nor did he believe that conceiving would put her at any greater risk than it did other women. He did, however, think the conception of a child was unlikely.

The odds against him, Darcy decided to embark upon the greatest gamble of his and his wife's lives. Indeed, he was gambling with his wife's life. Was it any wonder such night terrors plagued him?

After hearing from the physician, Darcy called on Mrs Clark in London. She had become his co-conspirator, and he would pay her generously for it, even more than had been promised for her to become his mistress. She was troubled by the deception, which he thought spoke well of her character.

"I can certainly understand and appreciate your hesitation," he told her. "Indeed, a ready agreement would have alarmed me more. But you must understand I cannot do this. It is in every manner abhorrent to me, to the vows I made to her. I love her too much to... No. It cannot even be spoken aloud."

Mrs Clark had been silent as she watched him struggle with his thoughts.

"She is correct in that not having a child has driven a wedge between us that it seems we cannot surmount," he said at last. "I know not what else we might do."

"What if you are wrong?" Mrs Clark asked him gently. "Then...?"

He could only shake his head and say, "I refuse to be wrong."

Now, some months hence, he stood in Italy with his wife slumbering in their bed some feet away, and he dared to dream that maybe... just maybe... he *had* been right. Perhaps the gamble would work.

His gaze traced her figure, stopping at a point just below where he knew her navel to be—a spot he had caressed and kissed, a spot she had clutched in agony too many times to be counted. Looking at that region, he offered up a silent prayer then whispered, "If you are in there, my child, pray stay with us and grow strong."

He then moved to his wife's beautiful countenance, feeling that clench in his heart that had been present since that autumn in Herefordshire, when Cupid's arrow had lodged itself so firmly within him. *Whatever happens,* he prayed, *let me not lose her.*

Without being asked, Ana Santina began to bring Elizabeth a light breakfast in her bed, to be eaten before ever she dared stir. The meal consisted of a dense sort of bread she called *focaccia,* studded with figs and rosemary and drizzled with honey. With it she brought a tea of sorts—it was nothing like the tea drunk in England, to be sure, but a brew that tasted of blood oranges and anise. Elizabeth made a face the first time she tasted it, not being overly fond of anise, but she could not deny that its effect on her stomach was remarkably soothing.

Given that she had decided to hide her illness from her husband, *something* remarkable was required. It was a mercy, she had decided, ignoring the inherent deception; he could not fear what was unknown to him. If she had any faith in herself for being able to carry it through—if it even was as she suspected—she would have told him. However, it simply could not be and thus would only lead to consternation and distress.

Elizabeth began forcing herself to appear lively—even when she was anything but—and to carry on cheerfully even as she looked around surreptitiously for a likely spot to toss up her accounts if needed. She dragged herself from her bed when she would have much rather slept, and she denied naps even when they were desired above all things.

Mrs Clark had confided in her the day prior that she had just had her courses again. Elizabeth had known already, thanks to the faithful Ana Santina, but appreciated Mrs Clark's open honesty. Any disappointment she might have felt over that was second, however, to her concerns for her own state.

She spent some time contemplating when her last courses had afflicted her, unable to come to any satisfactory conclusion. How much easier it might have been if they had brought her maid! But they had not wished any of the household to know what they were up to, and so they engaged local servants to help them. The very best that she could determine was that it had perhaps been June but maybe was July. Then again, it might have been May. It was not at Rosings; but this was her only certainty. In truth, after years of watching and waiting and hoping for the absence of her courses, it had been refreshing to be able to disregard them entirely.

Her thoughts tended there one sunny afternoon while she and Mrs Clark sat out sketching on the piazza. Mrs Clark, in addition to her many other uses, was an excellent artist and was helping Elizabeth to capture the sights of their journey. She had shown Elizabeth some techniques, a few little tricks to employ, and Elizabeth could not deny that it was leading to some far more creditable work than she had ever produced before.

"What was around the time of your birthday?" Mrs Clark asked, pulling Elizabeth from the calculations in her mind.

Elizabeth startled, having not realised she spoke aloud. Mrs Clark had paused in her endeavour and sat, her charcoal poised above the pad, regarding her in a friendly way. For a moment, Elizabeth wondered if she should confide in her, but another moment persuaded her she ought not to. Under no circumstances could Darcy find out about this possibility. If he knew... No, under no circumstances could her husband learn of this. She was convinced that the only reason he continued to come to her bed was that she had at last made him believe she could not conceive again. If he knew she had and therefore could again, they would return to the way things were in the spring, the dreadful, dark springtime.

"Um, a fortnight prior to my birthday is my sister

Jane's birthday." Elizabeth turned her attention to her own sketch, busily shading in the face of one of the buildings. "I was just thinking about what I had given her for a present and wondering whether she had found it useful."

"I am sure she must have," said Mrs Clark, smiling warmly. "What was it?"

Elizabeth continued shading, her mind having gone utterly blank. She and Jane were never much in the habit of purchasing gifts for one another. Jane used to say that her favourite birthday present ever was when she was two and received a sister—Elizabeth herself.

"Ah, it was... ah, a tonic. A beauty tonic. Jane worries about losing her bloom."

"I see," said Mrs Clark.

Lapsed into silence again, Elizabeth returned to her own thoughts. If her calculations were true, it could be that nearly four months had passed since the last time she had her courses. *That cannot be correct*, she told herself, *for if it is...*

But she had been quite far along for the last, most dreadful miscarriage. That was why it had been so hard on her; it was why she had nearly died. Cold fear suddenly struck her heart as the reality of her situation, the possibility that she might die here, truly struck her.

Hard on the heels of that grim thought came another. If she died, and Darcy had conceived a child with Mrs Clark—would he marry *her*? A cold sweat broke out over her skin at the very thought, and she turned her head such that her gasping breath would go unheard by Mrs Clark.

She mostly kept these thoughts at bay, her darker

feelings regarding this alliance she and Mrs Clark had made, but now they rushed at her. Half-thought images of tangled limbs, of Darcy's voice whispering endearments in Mrs Clark's ear—*he would not do that, Lizzy, stop!* she scolded herself—and then Mrs Clark taking her place in London and at Pemberley. Elizabeth herself had set it up so that it would be easy enough to do. Darcy would not be the first widower to turn to his wife's friend for shared sorrow and then a shared bed. In this case, the shared bed would have come first and by her own blessing!

She was suddenly on her feet, dropping the charcoals which had been in her hand. "Ex-Excuse me, Mrs Clark," she said before turning back towards their apartments, fortunately only steps away.

"Are you well?" Mrs Clark called after her, but Elizabeth refused to hear her. No, she was not well, not well at all.

Darcy found walking through the streets of Rome to be a charming diversion on an afternoon. He often stopped in the markets to find some treat or another and sought out picturesque little corners and nooks to show to his wife during later jaunts.

Having returned from just such an endeavour, he came upon Mrs Clark sitting out on the piazza, having apparently been sketching.

After greeting her, he said, "I am surprised I do not

find Mrs Darcy with you. Such a fine day, one would not expect her to be indoors."

"She was here until about a quarter of an hour ago," Mrs Clark said. Then, after a measured pause, she added, "She was required to return indoors rather suddenly. I would have gone after her, but I think she desired solitude."

Darcy gestured towards the bench that she occupied, and Mrs Clark nodded. "Was she upset about what she believes is ongoing?"

"She might have been." Mrs Clark frowned, considering, then added, "She is as yet unwell. She looks tired all the time."

"She does." Darcy swallowed to quell the little thrill of excitement that thought incited. "And yet, she says nothing of any malady to me."

"Nor I. I asked her one morning if she felt ill, and she flatly denied it, though I daresay I heard her only minutes earlier." She looked at him and said, "No doubt she cannot bear the thought of disappointing you."

"In truth, I do not think I could bear another disappointment," he acknowledged. "We must keep her in good spirits, above all."

"Yes," said Mrs Clark. "I could not agree more."

"I will speak to her, determine if there is any distress. Perhaps you might ask after her health?"

Mrs Clark agreed, and the plan was settled.

As he had indicated to Mrs Clark, Darcy invited Elizabeth to take a moonlit stroll in the Piazza Navona later that evening. For whatever had sent her flying indoors earlier that day, she seemed in her customary good humour that evening. They had all three dined together, and Elizabeth had shared with them the news that her sister Kitty had of late delivered a son. Kitty had married the parson at Kympton so this news was of interest for more than one reason.

"Mrs Reynolds shall see to it that they are comfortable, I hope?" Darcy asked.

"She has already done it," Elizabeth replied. "Her letter came directly after that of our brother Mathers. He is well pleased with his boy, to be sure." She said the last with a smile, and Darcy knew his wife felt genuine pleasure in the event.

The evening was warm; late September in Italy did not bring with it a nip in the air as it did in England. Many people were out on the streets on such an evening as this, and Darcy found he rather enjoyed the bustle and noise of it all.

From his peripheral vision, he saw Elizabeth yawn, raising her hand hurriedly to cover her mouth. She saw that he had noticed and ended her yawn with a laugh. "Forgive me, darling."

It gave him the ideal opening. "You have been rather tired of late, have you not? I hope our travels have not exhausted you."

"No, not at all," she said immediately. "In fact, I have almost been sleeping too well."

He laughed. "How is that possible?"

"I find myself having the strangest dreams," she told him. "They wake me out of sleep sometimes, they are so exceedingly odd."

"Oh? Such as what?"

"I dreamt that Lady Catherine and I were swimming in the sea together," she said. "She did not think I was proficient and scolded me that I ought to practise more. Then I dreamt that I had a kitten, and it disliked me and tried to claw and bite me."

"Good heavens," Darcy said with a laugh. "Strange dreams indeed!"

"I dreamt I was in Paris and could not speak to anyone. All knowledge of French had deserted me, and no matter what I tried to say to them, it came out as jabber. I declare, they rather make me doubt my sanity sometimes!"

Again, the last was said with a smile—she did not seem to have any true anxiety over it—and so Darcy smiled back. Then, with greater gravity, he said, "Italy does not agree with you, I fear."

"The food is very different," she said. "Perhaps I must only accustom myself to different tastes and spices."

"Perhaps so," he agreed. "Though I wonder..."

She looked up at him.

"Maybe it is less Italy itself than our reason for being here? Perhaps it begins to weigh on you."

She was quiet for a moment; the moon shed just enough light for her to cast her countenance into shadow, and Darcy wished she would look more directly at him so that he could see the expression in her eyes. At last, she asked, "Should it?"

"Of course not." He paused and, after glancing around, pulled her into his arms. This was one of the things he enjoyed about Italy. If a man felt like embracing his wife on the street, no one had anything to say about it.

She rested against his chest, not looking at him.

Tender feeling washed over him, and the sensation was almost painful. "You know I love you more today than even the day I proposed to you."

She looked up, her chin now touching his cravat. "Which time?"

"Both," he murmured. "It has been many years now that I have loved you ardently. Anything, everything I do is for that cause, that you might have complete joy."

"And I for you," she replied in a soft voice. "I want you to be happy."

Such a peculiar circumstance they were in! Each of them with their own secrets and deceits yet bound together for the cause they pursued together, each in their own way. He did feel his guilt in the matter and could only pray that if things turned out as he believed they would—nay, as he *knew* they would—she would be so happy that she would not resent him for it.

When would they admit their truths to one another? He believed, more with each day, that she had likely conceived, and yet she said nothing. She hid her struggles from him, admitting to nothing.

She pulled away, afflicted by another enormous yawn. He smiled and said, "Let us get you to your bed."

CHAPTER TEN

THE SUGGESTION
OF HOPE

Sunrise in Rome was gentle, even if the sun itself was so much brighter than in Derbyshire or London. In October, the slight chill in the air made for ideal sleep. Elizabeth often found herself abed until the sun was rather high in the sky, the warm rays pressing against her eyelids and the fluffy white bed linens soft against her skin.

Every single day, as she woke, before she even opened her eyes, she found herself taking stock of things. Did she feel as though her courses might have started? No. Did she feel as if they might start? No. Did she have cramps? No.

Did she feel the first flutters of life within her womb? Also no.

For the last, she never knew whether to be relieved or dismayed. She reminded herself with regularity that what was not gained could not be lost. It had happened too many times before not to happen this time too. Furthermore, it could be—likely would be?—deadly to her. It would do her much better to not be pregnant at all than to have conceived and suffer the loss of it.

There is no hope, Elizabeth, and you would do best to remember it.

But hope, wretched hope, would spring like a flower emerging from the stony ground of her heart. *What if this time, it could be different?*

Elizabeth opened her eyes to find Darcy had entered her bedchamber. They were not sharing a bed in Italy, for practical purposes, but it did not follow that he was banned from entering. He wore a queer expression as he looked at her, and she said, "What is it?"

He shook his head. "How do you feel?"

"Perfectly well," she said, a bit tartly. She pulled herself into a seated position. "How do *you* feel?"

"I am well." But he sounded grave and thoughtful, not well at all.

"What is it? Why were you looking at me like that?"

He crossed the room slowly and took a seat at the edge of her bed. "You were... holding yourself."

"What? *Holding* myself?"

He studied her for another minute before saying, "Your, um, your hand was on your... your stomach. You seemed as though you were..."

Elizabeth's stomach lurched. She looked past him, towards the window and the sunshine. "I was asleep, and I knew not what I did."

"Do you not think that after these many years I do not know the pattern of your breath when you sleep as compared to when you are awake?"

She laughed uncomfortably. "What do you accuse me of?"

He rose and walked around the room slowly, seeming like he was looking for something, but if he did, he did not find it. "The only time I have ever seen you do that is when… when…"

"When what?"

"When you were with child."

She laughed, and it was nearly a cackle. "Lest you forget, sir, I cannot conceive."

"According to one doctor."

"A doctor who is correct. We have been married five years!"

"Elizabeth…"

"What? What do you want me to say?" She swung her legs over the bed, quickly rising, then retrieved her dressing gown with a dramatic flourish from the chair where she had placed it the night prior. "We have not… that is to say, if you recall, I said we must abstain while you were… involved with Mrs Clark—"

"I am not *involved* with Mrs Clark," he said with unmistakable hauteur in his voice. "And yes, while you and I have abstained for some time, it has not been so long that it would be impossible for you to be increasing."

"Do not concern yourself with my womb, sir, not unless you have already succeeded in the business which has brought us here."

Darcy's face went pale, and he stared at her.

"How goes it, husband? What of our child, in the womb which will welcome and nurture it?" Anger made Elizabeth feel hot and itchy all of a sudden, but she could not give in. With one large step, she was toe to toe, glaring up at him. "Tell me, what of that?"

"I will not speak to you of that."

"Then we have nothing much more to say," she said. "I am not capable of bearing your child. I would give the world if I could, but I cannot. So do not concern yourself with me; your energies must be devoted to her."

He took a step away from her and then turned his back on her, leaving the room moments later.

Elizabeth sank back down onto her bed, hot fat tears coursing down her cheeks as she rocked back and forth, crying and crying. She cried until her throat was raw, and her face was swollen and red, and then she merely sat, numb with the grief and frustration which had led her there.

A detached part of her recognised that the quarrel they had just had was perhaps not equal to her display of sorrow. She marvelled at her histrionics even as she luxuriated in them. Darcy would come to her later, his anger dissipated. They would kiss, they would forgive; and yet, indulging herself in this display of sensibility felt too good to forgo. She wanted to wail and scream and kick, even if she was not wholly sure why.

When the tears had at last subsided, and Elizabeth had wiped her face clean with a cool cloth, she had another precipitous realisation. The sickness had gone. She had nearly leapt from her bed, walked around, sat, stood, laid... and all the while, it was well. There was no sense that her stomach might flip, no metallic taste in her mouth, no queasy uncertainty. Furthermore, she felt her usual energies. A long ramble through the streets seemed not only enticing but possible. She was wholly prepared to greet the day with an enthusiasm she had not felt for some weeks now.

It is done.

The understanding of what that meant sank into her heart. It was done, then, whatever brief flicker of life had illuminated within her. Gone now.

She knew how this would be. It had happened to her before. The sickness passed and within days, pain began. Pain and blood, Eve's curse made manifest within her. She sighed.

And what to tell Darcy?

She had no wish to frighten or alarm him, nor did she wish to endure his sorrow atop her own. She could not bear to see the look in his eyes. He would think her dying, and she... well, perhaps she would die. What would it do to him to watch it? It had marked him considerably before, living through Georgiana's death and then her near-death. Would it not be a mercy to him to spare him that fear? If it was meant to happen, he could not stop it, and if it did not happen, there was no use making him worry over it, nor grieve what she lost.

I must send him off until I can get through this.

Darcy left their residence and began an aimless perambulation of the streets, agitated and dismayed by the exchange he had just had with his wife. His introduction of the subject had not been fully intentional; yes, it was a topic on which there was much that needed said, but he had not wanted, ought not to have dared, to broach it in that moment. When he entered—seeking a book he believed her done with—and saw her cradling her lower abdomen, the promise of it had overwhelmed his reason.

Now he was left to roam the streets, left to the satisfaction of forcing her to say that which he did not wish to hear. But what had she said exactly? She had not denied it, did she? She had merely diverted his attention, speaking of their marital relations and then the goal which brought them to Italy.

Do not concern yourself with my womb, sir, not unless you have already succeeded in the business which has brought us here.

He exhaled forcibly, causing a passing woman to look at him curiously. What she might do—how she might feel!—if she knew there was *no* possibility in that quarter? Succeeded in the business? No, he had refused to undertake the business outright.

Everything that he had thought, and felt, and done, had depended on his belief that if only the strain of duty was relieved, she would conceive. *I refuse to be wrong* —those were the words he said to Mrs Clark. But it was not so easy, was it? Had not life taught him that much at least, that very little of it was within his control?

"You are still an arrogant, selfish idiot," he muttered. "Still in want of humbling, to be sure."

A woman knows her body, she had told him once; was he still so pompous that he imagined he knew better than she? Yes, he had. He had discounted her notions of womanly comprehension, believing that he understood the nervous strain she was under and how it affected her, even if she did not.

A fine sweat came over him as he considered that. Had his high-handedness defeated him once again? For a moment, he considered going back to her bedchamber and confessing everything. Would she forgive him? Would she ever trust him again? He had deceived her, telling himself that the ends justified the means.

But if there was no good end to it, then he could hardly expect her clemency, could he?

He had come to the fountain and stood a moment, looking at Neptune spearing the octopus. Though he hardly believed in old superstitions and the myths of ancient times, Neptune, the god of fertility, had seemed an auspicious overseer of their work, most particularly because he stood with the octopus. The octopus, some believed, was the harbinger of creativity, a creature that was outside of what was conventional and expected.

Now Darcy thought the statue may be perceived otherwise. Neptune was *spearing* the octopus; perhaps Darcy should have seen it as a sign that in matters of fertility, it was best to keep to what was expected and usual, the methods by which children had come to bear since the dawn of man.

What he did not know was where to go from here. He could not be certain that Elizabeth was—or was not —with child. He knew not what to do if she was not. Confess all? Uphold the agreement in the manner Elizabeth believed he had done all along? There were no clear answers; above all he wanted for time to contemplate and form his own schemes.

"Naples," Elizabeth said brightly at dinner. "Do you not wish to see the excavations at Pompeii?"

They had been careful with each other all afternoon. Darcy had been absent from Elizabeth's company for several hours, and when he returned, he said nothing of where he had been.

"I do," he replied, his attention on his plate. "But I had thought we should go together."

"No, I would prefer you went without me," she told him. "I really have no interest in it. Seems rather frightening, in fact. All those people burnt up without warning."

He looked at her oddly. She had never before exhibited any sort of squeamishness, and it no doubt seemed out of character that she should do so now. But he did not question that, instead choosing to take some issue with the time required.

"It is nearly three days there and three back. In order to see them properly, I daresay I should be gone eight days, maybe more."

Perfect. "Take a fortnight," she suggested. "I will be perfectly happy to be quiet and alone in that time."

"Alone? Well, you would have Mrs Clark."

"No, you will." On his look, she insisted, "Darcy, she should go with you."

"Elizabeth, I cannot be seen—"

"No one cares!" Elizabeth exclaimed. "The Italians all have mistresses. They will think me a better wife for permitting you yours."

"She is not my—" Darcy stopped himself, breathing hard.

Elizabeth leant over the table. "She is, though, is she not?"

A storm of emotion played over his face. She hardly understood it. Grief, fear, longing, anger... They were all there. She found herself both afraid and in awe of him.

He remained silent for long, excruciatingly slow minutes. At last, he rose.

"I have said it from the beginning, and I repeat it now. She is not my mistress, nor should she be perceived as such." He bowed. "She stays here."

He turned to leave the room, and Elizabeth rose with such rapidity that she nearly toppled her chair. "Do not dare think to quit this room, Fitzwilliam Darcy!"

He turned to her in no little astonishment, and she recognised how she sounded—disrespectful, shrewish, even a bit silly. *Like a fishmonger's wife*, she thought, *or my mother*. The thought nearly made her burst out in nervous, unrestrained laughter. But no; laughter at this time would be wrong. She and her husband were having a row, the second of that day. She took a deep breath, steering her temper into more rational seas.

"We came here for a purpose," she reminded him, more gently. "A child. I hope you have not forgotten."

His dark eyes studied her intently. "No, I have not forgotten."

"Have you not? It seems to me, at times, that I am the only person who really wants this."

"How could you think so?" he asked. "How can you doubt my wishes?"

Elizabeth did not know. All she did know was that the tide of emotion within her was rising again, uncontrollable even as she wished to control it. "Then take her with you," she said. "Let us not waste a moment, certainly not a fortnight."

"You ask too much," he said.

"I know you have not succeeded with her. She is not increasing as yet, and we have already been at this several months!"

Elizabeth began then to cry, falling back into her chair and covering her face with her hand. Darcy sprang to her side in a trice, pulling her into an embrace as best he could from the chair beside her.

"Do not doubt me. I want it more than almost anything, for myself and for you both," he murmured into her hair. "The only thing I want more is for you to be happy."

"This situation is obviously wearing on us both," she sobbed. "Take her. Take some days with her out of my sight, out of my hearing, out of my knowledge. I beg you."

"Elizabeth, you—"

"It is so very hard," she choked. "So very hard to pretend I do not mind when I do mind. I mind a great deal. It should be me, and yes, I do recall that this entire scheme was my idea, but it does not mean that I cannot despise it at times."

He sighed, and the warmth of his breath stirred her curls. At last, he said, "I think it will not be very long now."

"How can you say so?"

"I just... I believe it to be so. I feel it in my heart."

Elizabeth grew still. She had wondered, after that morning, if he perceived any alteration in her. She could not let him think it. She refused to allow him to sway, believing that she had triumphed over her faulty body in some manner.

She would lose this small bit of whatever within her. She knew that. So why not tell him it had already happened, spare him whatever little hope that morning had granted him?

She pulled away from him, using the handkerchief he gave her to wipe her face. With careful authority, she told him, "If whatever you believed you saw this morning has given you some notion of an achievement on my end, pray discard it at once."

"I have never seen you in any such posture save when—"

"'Twas but a dream. Nothing more."

"But—"

"My love." She placed her hand on his. "It is in every way impossible. Pray believe me."

Their gazes met, and she saw as he stared then doubted and eventually accepted her words.

"Go," she urged. "Take her with you."

He was gone in the morning, taking only his man with him. About an hour later, Mrs Clark and her trunk were placed within a separate carriage, and they left too. Elizabeth hoped, rather than believed, she was en route to Naples.

She sat at the window overlooking the piazza for many long hours, feeling as alone as she ever had in her life.

CHAPTER ELEVEN

SUCH TREMBLINGS & FLUTTERINGS

I t happened on the fourth day that Darcy was gone.

Elizabeth lay in her bed, having just awoken; in retrospect, she wondered if perhaps what happened was what caused her to wake, for it was only just dawn, the sun casting rosy-hued fingers towards her window. It was a peculiar trembling and fluttering, a part of her and yet separate from her, rising from deep within. Her hand flew to her abdomen, and she exclaimed loudly, surprised and delighted.

It stopped at once. Had she imagined it? She was as still as she could be, waiting and praying and hoping. Just as soon as she had resolved to herself that it had been nothing more than her imagination, it happened again, stronger and surer. Though she had never felt anything like it before, somehow she knew exactly what it was.

Tears sprang to her eyes, elation commingled with dismay. "Oh no," she said, her voice shaking. "Oh my dear… oh, no, no, pray do not make me love you. No, no, it will be so much worse, oh no."

It was too late. She was in love as she had never loved before, even as she warned herself not to become attached to this little butterfly baby of hers. She carefully splayed both hands across her abdomen, wishing that he or she might feel her love and protection, praying that it would somehow help it cling to its nascent life.

"Do not leave me," she whispered. "Pray, stay with me. Cling on, my little one. Cling tightly to me. We will get through it together."

Fear immobilised her. She remained in her bed all that day, refusing the assistance of Ana Santina, who bustled in looking for illness but left muttering *"bambino"* under her breath and smiling in a self-satisfied way. Elizabeth could not eat, nor sleep, nor read; she only lay or sat, feeling the sensations within her, such as the child chose to grace her with.

To sleep that night terrified her. What if it was all done when she woke? But the next day she woke in the same manner of the day prior, in the pink of dawn with a new life tumbling about within her. "Good morning, my beloved," she murmured. "How good of you to stay with me another day."

Elizabeth resolved that she would chronicle this wonder within her. Inasmuch as she could not yet believe it real, hope, like a particularly stubborn fever, had infected her. Her words would be addressed to her husband; if by some miracle they would one day hold this child in their arms, she wished for him to know of these early, heady hours of existence.

I hope you will forgive me when you know what I have done. Since coming to Italy, I have been hiding something, a very small something which has taken up residence within me. Oh, that wretched doctor of ours!—for it seems he was quite incorrect, and I have been able to conceive after all.

It began as the most delicious little movements within me, like a fairy blowing bubbles. How I do wish that I might share them with you! Alas, such is the lot of a man. As ladies, we know our children for many months before our husbands do, but then again, we also know the travail of bearing them. I suppose this is our reward, then.

I only pray that he lives to meet you.

On the sixth day of Darcy's absence, an older maid with the air of a *nonna* arrived bearing an enormous tray of pastas and meats, and on cue, Elizabeth's stomach growled fiercely. The woman stood, hands tucked into the apron which stretched across her middle, and smiled, murmuring approvingly while Elizabeth ate.

It was a veritable bounty, what the *nonna* brought, and yet somehow Elizabeth ate and ate and still wanted more. Fortunately, the Italian ladies liked nothing more than feeding her. Over the next day came a multitude of trays bearing every manner of good thing, and with the trays appeared a bountiful array of older ladies who stood over her clucking happily while she devoured it all.

There was but one thing on the trays she could not

contemplate, and that was the milk. Ana Santina believed—as did her maid at Pemberley—that there were innumerable benefits in a glass of milk for a lady in a delicate state. Elizabeth had always obliged her maid at Pemberley, but here in Italy, she could not. Though her nausea had abated, and her overall vigour was returned, the idea of milk still made her stomach clench and flip in protest, and Ana Santina was put off more easily than was Dylan.

Elizabeth soon felt as though indolence was driving her mad, so she eventually gained the courage to rise from her bed. Relief swept through her when she did not instantly begin to miscarry. She walked to the window with slow careful steps, telling herself how silly she was to behave so and yet unable to stop it. There was a comfortable chair by the window with a perfect view of the piazza, and she happily imagined a day of watching people going about their lives outside.

She kept a book on her lap all day, but she never opened it. The day was crisp and bright, and everyone appeared inclined to enjoy it. Children ran and played, and adults formed and re-formed little knots of society, their conversation and laughter filling the air. The environment outside was like one large, ever-changing party, and part of her longed to be among them even as another part realised how pleasant it was to observe the gaiety. She described it all to her own little bambino, fancying that sometimes she felt movement in reply to her voice.

Elizabeth kept up her post for several days, enjoying the impromptu little theatre before her. So many intriguing characters for her study! There was a little girl who reminded her so much of Lydia in her girlhood, all ribbons and flounces and impertinence. Then there was an old lady, small and round and gnarled with age, wearing no cover on her head but a purple and red scarf; obviously, she was a long-lost countess of some distant land or another. Elizabeth imagined fantastic stories for nearly everyone she saw, weaving tales of foreign lands and intrigues to share with her little fluttering butterfly, who sent up occasional twitters to let her know he was enjoying them. These, too, she shared in her journal for Darcy each day, feeling strengthened in the surety that he would one day have the felicity of reading it.

Our son will be an avid reader. Of this I am certain. He delights in these little stories I concoct. How happy will be the day that he is able to avail himself of Pemberley's library!

On the eleventh day of Darcy's absence, Elizabeth again woke with the dawn, her dear little bambino being restless and enjoying some little game of kick and punch within her. She lay there for several pleasurable minutes, revelling in the sensations. "You are well," she whispered in amazed tones. "I feel you, my little one. Perhaps you will not like to read after all, for you will be too busy running and jumping and inventing mischief."

Elizabeth wrote to Darcy at least thrice each day; some guilt for her deception had come upon her, particularly because she imagined him on a desultory trudge through the ruins, likely feeling the dismay brought about by his suspicions. She did her best to describe each jostle and poke within her and also availed herself of the opportunity to renew those loving affirmations to him which had once flowed so easily from her lips. It was easy to say so to him; knowing that this part of him was within her filled her with grateful, loving ardour. She felt very much like a blushing bride again, though her bridegroom was absent, and their marriage was of some years' duration.

She began to yearn for his return and even to anticipate the happy surprise she had for him.

Darcy had been gone a fortnight when the trouble began. Elizabeth, having grown restive with even the delights afforded by watching the piazza, decided she would venture to take a short walk. Ana Santina dressed her with care and asked if she might accompany her. "I do not think it necessary," she told her. "A slow stroll around la Fontana, that is all. I will be returned before you can even think to miss me."

She moved slowly and carefully, but her usual pace soon asserted itself, and she had to remind herself to slow down, to take care. Nevertheless, she had nearly returned to their apartments when from seemingly nowhere, a bolt of pain shot through her lower abdomen and legs. She cried out, halting immediately.

For a moment she stood frozen in place, terror afflicting every part of her, from her shaking hands to her pounding heart and quivering knees. The pain subsided, but she was not so silly as to think herself in the clear.

Another step proved her correct. The pain shot through her once more. She did not cry out this time, but tears sprang to her eyes, not of pain but of the grief to come. "No, no, little one," she whispered. "You have done very well so far. Stay with me, I beg you."

She made it back into her apartment, laying herself down, shoes and all, on her bed. As long as she was motionless, all was well, but the slightest movement brought back her agony.

Ana Santina arrived in the midst of one miserable pang; there might have been a difference between them in terms of the language they called their own, but the language of women needed no words to be spoken. One look at her mistress's pale face and teary eyes told Ana Santina everything she needed to know. She immediately hurried from the room.

Elizabeth knew not where the maid went but sensed that help, or at least an attempt at it, was on its way. If she could have felt relief, she would have, but she doubted too much that anything could be done but to comfort her, to utter those nonsense words that never meant anything: *"You are young. You still have time. It will happen. Just relax."*

At least this time they will be in Italian. That, at least, will be some new addition to the dreadful ritual.

Ana Santina returned with two women; one of them was very old and very small, her tiny face wrinkled like a little dried apple with wisps of white hair escaping her headscarf. The other lady was not as old and not as small but carried with her an air of assuredness. Elizabeth knew instinctively to trust them and willingly turned her body and the life within it over to them.

Ana Santina, who had the most English, urged her to permit them to examine her. She first undressed Elizabeth and put her into a nightgown of superfine muslin. The maid then spent a great deal of time situating her among the fluffy white pillows, draping the bed linens just so to preserve her modesty, although in truth, Elizabeth hardly cared. Her modesty was the least of her concerns, and she truly felt she might have permitted anyone to touch her anywhere if it would save the child within her.

The oldest lady went first, pushing and prodding and murmuring rapidly to the other two. Elizabeth could not understand even a word of the conversation that flew amongst the three women, their hands moving almost as quickly as their tongues. They touched her everywhere, sometimes gently, sometimes not, but did not content themselves with that. They listened to her heart and even put an ear to her stomach; at one point the oldest of them even appeared to be smelling her. In other circumstances, Elizabeth might have been amused or embarrassed, but in these, she was only fearful, mentally willing them to fix it.

At last, Ana brought her a bowl of water and asked Elizabeth to wash herself with it. After an uncertain glance at the other two, she did, cleansing herself once, twice, and then a third time on the maid's urging. When Ana Santina was satisfied, she took the used water and handed it to the other two ladies. The not-quite-as-old woman held it while the other took a little phial of olive oil from her many dark skirts and dribbled some over the top. They watched it intently.

Elizabeth found herself holding her breath, though she had no idea what was happening or why. Her gaze shifted between the bowl and the ladies, all three intent on the bowl of water, just waiting and watching for something Elizabeth knew nothing about.

Then the oldest lady broke into a large smile, and a cheer rose among the women. Elizabeth released her breath in a gasp, tears springing to her eyes as she was hugged and kissed and chattered at, the most prevalent word amongst them being, "*Due!*"

"*Due?*" she asked. "Two? What does it mean, two? And why am I having pains? Is the baby well?"

"The pains," explained Ana Santina while the other two gathered up their things, "are the stretches of the womb. The bambinos, they are two, and they grow very fast now. The womb must grow faster than it like sometimes. It will happen many times, but it is only the stretch. Not to be worried. In *febbraio* they will be in your arms."

It was hard to comprehend all the feelings within Elizabeth at such words. Elation, yes, but still fear. But mostly elation. She had scarcely any time to think of it, though, for at that moment, a man's voice came from the doorway. "Mrs Darcy, what is the meaning of all of this?"

Darcy had returned.

CHAPTER TWELVE

TAUGHT TO HOPE

The two older ladies still lingered. Darcy, though he knew not why they were there exactly, did comprehend what it was they wanted from him. With no hesitation, he pressed a handful of coins into their palms, causing them to thank him profusely and murmur blessings and instructions he had no comprehension of. All the while, his eyes were fixed on his wife and his wife's on his.

As soon as the room was clear of everyone but the two of them, he came to her, who lay in the bed, and took a seat on the edge of her mattress. He took one of her hands in his left hand then bowed his head and pressed his right hand to his forehead, his eyes closed. Elizabeth watched him draw a very deep breath. She wondered what he was thinking, if he was angry, suspecting she had misled him and sent him away.

When he raised his head, the raw emotion in his eyes smote her. It was times like these that she knew how he loved her; he would never be given to pretty speeches, her Darcy, but his eyes would always say what she needed to know.

He leant towards her and kissed her on the forehead, then her cheek, and then her lips. Then he rested his forehead on hers and asked, "Are you well?"

"I am," Elizabeth said in a half sob. "I am well."

He pulled back, regarding her with tenderness that made her heart ache. "We will get through this, my love. We will."

"I... I have a confession to make. I have not been completely honest with you."

"I know," he said. "I have suspected... this."

Elizabeth's confession tumbled from her lips in a rush. "My courses have not come for some months, and then, you know I have not been feeling well, and I told you it was the food, but I knew it was different, and before, whenever I have felt sick, the end of the sickness always meant pain and... and misery...they were not far behind. So when I felt better, a little above a fortnight ago, I imagined that it meant another miscarriage was nigh."

This was evidently a surprise to him. "About to miscarry, you sent me away? Elizabeth! What if you had died while I was gone?"

"I know and I pray you will forgive me." She took a deep breath, feeling a tear slip from her eyes. "But it does not signify, not now. I... I have felt him. Or her.

The baby has quickened. Those women were the midwives, and they felt him too."

Elizabeth saw his breath catch; like her, he had difficulty in allowing himself to hope. "But it is still early, yes?"

"Not so very early," she admitted. "And I have never felt a baby quicken before. Whatever I might have known or thought or felt in other pregnancies, the things I have been feeling are quite unlike anything I have ever known."

His hands reached for her, seemingly of their own volition, going towards the place beneath the coverlets where their child was at rest. She pushed the blankets aside, allowing Darcy to lay his hands on her lower abdomen. Emotion had turned his hands excessively warm, but it felt good. Alas, the child did not cooperate and make itself known to him.

"I do not feel movement," he admitted. "But you feel... different. More solid." Heartfelt delight diffused over his countenance—she had never seen him look thus —followed by a broad smile and then a chuckle before he removed his hands and cupped her face. "I hope she is your very image."

"He will look very strange if he looks exactly like me. Perhaps he will be tall, like you."

"Perhaps she will have your eyes."

"Perhaps he will have *your* eyes."

Giddy elation swept through her, and she saw the feeling mirrored in Darcy's countenance. It hearkened her back to that day in October when she had accepted his offer of marriage. They had stood that day, too, smiling, happy, brought back from the brink of misery into loving felicity with one another. In fact, she thought she might even feel better now than on that day.

"The midwives believe there are two," she told him.

"Then my joy is doubled as well. Perhaps there will be a boy and a girl."

"Perhaps there will," she agreed. "Although even just one is miracle enough for me."

Then, after a moment, she asked, very cautiously, "I suppose we might gain as many as three children from this endeavour?"

"Three?"

"Did not Mrs Clark attend you to Naples?" Elizabeth spoke lightly, not wishing to bestir any ill feeling.

"I have a confession of my own to make." She watched as he dropped his eyes and swallowed hard. "If Mrs Clark should happen to find herself with child, there should be no possibility that it would be my child."

"None?"

"None whatsoever."

Elizabeth knew not what to say about that. She had lies enough of her own in all of this, but he had set out wilfully to sink them, before ever they began.

"I see." She moistened her lips. "I suppose I can hardly chastise you for deception, not when—"

"Elizabeth." His eyes beseeched her. "How could you think for even a moment that I could lie with another woman, loving you as I do? You are my heart and my soul, dearest, loveliest Elizabeth, and the thought of another..." He shuddered. "It was beyond comprehending."

"But you said…" Her voice trailed away as she considered what it was, exactly, that Darcy had ever said about her scheme. Her mind raced through conversation after conversation as she realised that her husband had neatly sidestepped away from any decision, or any outright agreement with her plans. He had misled her, but outright lies had not fallen from his lips. He had never truly given his word, never actually admitted to relations with Mrs Clark.

Too many emotions swirled within her for her to sort them all out. Was she angry that he had denied them the one chance she believed they had? "Very well," she said, her voice shaking a little. "You have played a trick on me. But why? What if I had not fallen pregnant? Then what?"

"It was a risk," he owned. "An enormous risk, and I would never have taken it—never persisted in it—if I did not truly believe, with all of my heart, that with the anxiety gone, you would, in fact, conceive our child. You had your scheme, but I had mine as well. I knew I could never persuade you otherwise—"

"It was desperate measures. My failure—"

"*Our* failure."

"—affected everything." Her voice still trembled and broke. "You could scarcely be near me. We were very nearly strangers. Something had to be done, no matter how unholy or unorthodox it might have been."

"I have lived in fear that the experience you suffered with your miscarriage would happen again. It became easier if I did not caress the silk of your skin, did not feel your lips against mine; I prayed that in time I would learn to forgo those things because I could not bear to undertake those activities which might have led to your death."

"I did die," she told him. "Every day that you were cold or aloof, or removed was a little death to me."

"You looked, always, so frail. You seemed to eat less and less. You did not sleep... you were not yourself, in any manner. You did not tease me. You did not sing to me—I began to feel—"

He stopped, but she believed she had some idea of what he had been going to say. "You felt as if you had married your cousin Anne?"

"It was not that bad," he rejoined immediately. "But I did fear for what would become of you, if you would ever regain your liveliness or if I had taken it from you forever.

"In any case, once we devised this notion of a... a helper, you were altered. You ate, you sang, you walked... your cheeks were pink, and your eyes sparkled. I began to think we might be victorious. You would be less anxious and therefore not miscarry, and I would therefore not lose you. It was unconscionable of me to deceive you—I despise myself for doing so—but I did think it for the greater good."

From deep within Elizabeth, a faint tremor confirmed the veracity of his statement.

"So she is not, nor has ever been your mistress?"

"Elizabeth, I have taken my enemy as my brother for you, but I could not take another woman for you. Every feeling within me revolted against it."

He looked positively haunted, and Elizabeth felt herself softening towards him. No matter what, she knew this man loved her with every fibre of his being. He had gambled with their future, but he had won.

"Can you forgive me?" he asked.

Prejudice and misunderstanding had always been their bane. Where once they had been the happiest couple in the world, now they could become the happiest family in the world, but in order to do so, no anger could be permitted to linger.

"I do," she replied softly. "Will you forgive me for misleading you and sending you away?"

"I already have," he said.

Elizabeth caressed her stomach, wondering if she deceived herself in that she already felt it growing rounder. Darcy placed his hand over hers, and their eyes met. "I forbid you to die," he said in a husky whisper.

For some reason, his assertion made her grin. "Well, as Fitzwilliam once said, you do like to have your own way in things."

"You should have learnt long ago not to listen to *him*. The man gossips more than ten women put together." With his eyes fixed on her face, Darcy bent, placing a gentle kiss on her stomach. "This is your papa," he told her stomach. "Your mother and I already love you very much, but I shall demand obedience from you in all things, beginning with an order to stay as you are until you are properly grown."

In Italy, they had taken to enjoying their breakfast on a small table for two which was on a terrace overlooking the courtyard. The terrace had just enough sun to warm even the chilliest days and boasted a lightly fragranced air from the olive and fig trees below it. Darcy was pensive as they ate, and Elizabeth, pausing in her meal, asked him what troubled him.

"Nothing at all," he said. "My mind is agreeably engaged on two matters."

She smiled and asked, "Will you share them with me?"

"The first may not be a compliment to you," he said, "though for myself, I find it very pleasing indeed."

"Now my curiosity is definitely aroused," she said, reaching for another slice of focaccia. She took a bite and raised her brow, silently urging him to continue.

With a twinkle in his eye, he said, "Only that I have never seen you eat so much. You have certainly eaten more than I did. Indeed, Fitzwilliam, in his days of military training, did not eat as much as that at the breakfast table."

Elizabeth laughed, not at all alarmed by such an accusation. "Fitzwilliam, no matter what military exercise he might have undertaken, has not ever shared his skin with another person—nor have you. So be not alarmed by my preferences in dining, sir, for I am at the pleasure of another authority altogether."

"I am surely not alarmed," Darcy replied. "In fact, I am rather pleased by it. You look very well, my darling. Being a mother suits you admirably."

Elizabeth blushed and then thought it how lovely that he could still provoke her blushes this many years into marriage. That idea made her blush more. To distract herself, she asked, "What was the second thing?"

The second matter that Darcy contemplated—which Elizabeth had considered herself—was when they might return to England. "As I see it, we should either go now," he said, "or resolve ourselves to our child being born in Italy."

"I confess the idea of spending winter in warmer climes does appeal to me. Has there been a master of Pemberley born on the Continent as yet?"

"An excellent question." Darcy considered it a moment then said, "Not the master of Pemberley, but my grandmother was born in Paris."

They discussed then how Pemberley did in their absence; Darcy felt that all was well, and in any case, were they not caring for Pemberley's future even then? His steward and land agent could surely manage the rest.

"Then it is decided," she said. "We are fixed, for the present time, where we are. Shall we write to all our relations of the good news?"

Her words produced a smile from Darcy, who rose from the small table and laid his serviette on the plate in front of him. "I will return in a moment," he promised.

He was gone only a minute or so and returned bearing an enormous sheaf of papers. He handed them to Elizabeth, who exclaimed over his industry. "But husband, I must say," she remarked, "for a man who once earned the praise of a certain young lady at Netherfield for the evenness of his writing, this is not your finest effort. Your headmaster would not be pleased with such blotches and blots."

"I found myself more in charity with Bingley than ever before, as my feelings and ideas were flowing rather rapidly," Darcy admitted. "Too rapidly to be contained. But my joy was expressed in the writing of them, and I daresay the recipients will apprehend that. If they do not, well, hang them, then, for I do not care. A father has not much time for writing, you know."

Elizabeth paused in her perusal to spend a moment beholding him. His countenance held no little amount of pride when he uttered the last. *A father has not much time for writing...*

How long she had yearned for Darcy to own that blessed appellation, and now, he would. She reached for his hand, laying hers atop his. "You are going to be the perfect father."

"No," he said immediately. "I do not imagine I shall ever be perfect, but I am determined that he or she shall know of my love. I daresay if a child knows it is loved, the rest must surely work itself out?"

"I suppose we are going to find out, are we not? But I confess I am surprised—I imagined you should become the disciplinarian."

"Not at all," he said immediately. "Those unhappy tasks must be your lot. I want to sneak them biscuits from my pocket and lend my ear when they think you are being unreasonable."

That made her laugh heartily. "But you know I am never unreasonable!"

Darcy was not of a disposition to overflow with mirth—usually. However, he found himself singularly incapable of restraining his joy as he spent the next days with his wife. She was, again, the Elizabeth of old, teasing and sweet, good-humoured and charmingly argumentative.

However, it could not be denied that he had his concerns for her. She, too, was far more willing to be cautious than she had ever been before—the pains which had beset her from her walk to the fountain that day had frightened her. Bit by bit, they began some small excursions and engagements, always ready to fly back to the apartments to rest or keep her feet up as needed.

Yet, it was not needed. Elizabeth was vigorous and healthy and the babe—or babes, if the midwives were correct—grew stronger by the day.

Mrs Clark returned from her jaunts three days after Darcy had, and they sat her down immediately to tell her their good news. Her happiness for them was genuine and heartfelt, but she had one concern on Elizabeth's behalf.

"I pray you will forgive my part in the deception," she said, with one or two uneasy glances at Darcy. "I did believe, as your husband did, that it would work for the best for you."

"Pray do not make yourself uneasy," Elizabeth told her. "I am resolved myself to settle my thoughts on the joy of my condition and worry not over what might have happened, or not, to get me here."

As it stood, Mrs Clark had some extraordinary news of her own. During her little sojourn to the Italian seaside, she had been introduced to a man of good fortune, a minor count called Nellasperanza. He was a bold, gregarious sort, and Mrs Clark had found herself quite taken in by his facility in amusing her. "It has been some time since I have laughed as I do with Nellasperanza," she told Elizabeth. "I know not what, if anything, will come of it, but I enjoy his society. It is very good to feel that simple pleasure again."

Darcy, perhaps feeling something of a responsibility for Mrs Clark, insisted on meeting the gentleman. Nellasperanza was in some ways reminiscent of Sir William Lucas—perhaps not the cleverest of men but well-intentioned and genial and always ready with a smile. They had a pleasant dinner with him, during which it became very clear to Elizabeth that he was rather taken with Mrs Clark—and she with him.

They had explained to Nellasperanza that Mrs Clark was a companion to Mrs Darcy which he did not appear to quite comprehend. He believed them sisters at first, but at length they succeeded in teaching him that Mrs Clark had known them only a short while.

"Indeed, sir," said Darcy one evening when the two couples strolled the piazza, "we had only known her a day or so before she was employed to come with us here."

"*Nulla accade per caso,*" Nellasperanza replied, with a knowing smile and a little bow towards Mrs Clark.

"Nothing happens by chance?" Elizabeth translated.

"Indeed not," said Nellasperanza. "For it seems all is just as it was meant to be."

CHAPTER THIRTEEN

THE END OF THE BEGINNING

England had changed completely when the Darcys returned to it at the end of May, or possibly it was exactly the same and it was they who had altered. In any case, they entered the town house happier than they had ever passed through the doors before, Elizabeth holding her small bundle to her chest while Darcy rested his hand protectively against the small of her back.

Mrs Hobbs stood in the hall, tears in her eyes. "Welcome home, Mr and Mrs Darcy," she said, though she hardly spared them a glance. Elizabeth could easily perceive the dampness around her eyes, and though her arms reached for their wraps, Elizabeth fancied she could see the housekeeper's fingers itching to touch her son.

"Mrs Hobbs," she said, extending the bundle towards the lady, "may I present Master Henry Bennet Darcy to you?"

In the end it had been only one child after all, but given the size of him, Elizabeth could not be surprised that the midwives had mistaken him for two. Everything about their boy was round, from the curls on his head to the swell of his tummy and the sweet little toes that peeped beneath his gowns. Belatedly, Darcy informed her, "I should have mentioned I was rather chubby as a baby."

The name of their child had been no little source of consternation to them. Darcy was adamant that no matter what they chose, it must be something that Saye could not turn into an epithet. Elizabeth had liked George, but Darcy ruled it out immediately. "He shall call him King George, Prinny, Prissy... no, George is very nearly rife with possibilities for a mind like Saye's. Next idea?"

"What of Thomas?" she asked. "My father's name and your father's second—"

"He will call him 'Lobcock'," Darcy replied darkly.

"What? That is absurd. Why?"

"Because some men..." Darcy sighed. Elizabeth did not doubt he disliked speaking of such things with his wife. "Some men refer to a... a..." —he gestured towards his trousers— "in the natural state as a doubting Thomas or a lobcock. Saye will choose the more obvious of the words and call my boy 'Lobcock.'"

"Very well. What about Edward?"

"Ed... Bed-warmer, Nutmeg, Hedge Whore—"

Elizabeth privately thought her husband was rather

extending the reach of his imagination for some of these, but granted, Saye could be more imaginative than anyone else she knew. "What about Peter? Your uncle, the judge, is a—"

"Peter? Come, my love, surely even you can see the humour there." Darcy cast her a reproachful glance. "No Peter, no Harry, no John." Darcy considered briefly then added, "No Robert either. He will call him 'Rogering Robert', 'Round Mouth,' or something of the like."

Elizabeth threw up her hands, laughing helplessly. "We shall run out of names, darling. Perhaps Fitzwilliam —he cannot mock that."

Darcy had shaken his head ruefully. "Absolutely not. You cannot even begin to comprehend the names he has given me over these years, and I am certain he still has them all at the ready! Piss-Proud Fitz, Prick-William, Fitz the Flute... it does not even bear thinking about."

It had been dear Mrs Clark who had offered an idea to them. "My son was called Henry," she said, "and while I should never suggest so great a personage as your son be named for mine, it was always a name I felt partial to."

"Henry." They both liked it immediately; something about it felt quite right after all.

"Saye be hanged," Darcy vowed. "My son shall be Henry."

They were scarcely settled in the house an hour when the family came to call. Fitzwilliam's wife was increasing again and very near her confinement, but she ventured out regardless, her husband steering her about like a small ship. Mrs Hobbs was well prepared for young Basil, whose wild animal spirits had earned him a name wherever he visited. She watched closely while he peered suspiciously at his new cousin and then took him off to the kitchens with the promise of a biscuit.

Jane and Bingley arrived next; Jane brought with her one of the most exquisite little gowns Elizabeth had ever seen, and she sighed over its prettiness, even as she kissed her sister's cheek. "No one has ever equalled you with a needle, Jane."

"Aunt Jane!" her sister trilled in reply. "How very well that sounds!"

Elizabeth passed Henry, who was sleeping. "You have been an aunt long before now."

"I have," Jane agreed. "Nevertheless, this one is special to me."

Elizabeth smiled at that.

"But Lizzy, you must tell me all! Your letters made it all sound as if it was nothing, but being so far away, with not even a sister to attend you during your time!—it must have simply been dreadful!"

Elizabeth considered that. How could she tell Jane that Mrs Clark, possessor of their darkest secret, had become like a sister to her? How could she explain that Ana Santina, who had been her salvation in the dark days she believed all was lost, was as dear to her as any aunt? And how to describe the attachment she felt to the veritable army of *nonnas* with their gabbling speech and fearless poking and prodding, who were more a comfort to her than her own mother ever could have been?

"I confess that once the first part was over—the sickness and fear—it was all quite easy," she told her sister. "I had made some friends by then, and their assistance was invaluable."

After all the difficulties of her past, Providence had shown mercy to her in her time of travail. It was over so quickly, she was in the middle before she knew she had begun, and within minutes it seemed a boy was laid into her arms. The experience had not been so for Darcy who had been tugged out into the piazza by the menfolk of the neighbourhood. There he was made to play a white-lipped and silent game of bocce meant to distract him from the goings-on nearby. For him, her labours had lasted an eternity, much as he forgot them the instant he beheld his son.

"I was relieved it was only one and not two as the midwives believed," Elizabeth told her sister. "I daresay that would have made the business a bit trickier."

Bingley, who had gone to join the little knot of male exuberance when he entered, left them and came towards her. Bingley, Elizabeth knew, did not much like babies until they walked. He felt they were terrifyingly fragile before then and had no wish to be the source of a horrifying accident. True to form, he afforded Henry only a smile and a little salute before turning to Elizabeth.

"How did you find Lake Como? I understand you and Darcy took a little turn and stayed a fortnight."

"Not a fortnight complete, no," Elizabeth said with a little smile. It had come true after all, her long-cherished dream of standing on the shore of that magnificent lake with the future of Pemberley in her arms. "We found it to be utter perfection. I should recommend it heartily to anyone."

Saye entered with Lillian, and Elizabeth saw, with some surprise, that once again Lilly had a rounded stomach. An autumn child, she mused, then offered a smile. "A spare for Matlock?" she asked after they had greeted one another.

Lilly rolled her eyes and then said, "Put Henry to your *own* breast. I beg you. They say it delays things at least a little!"

"Hey-ho, Henry!" Saye cried out the moment he saw their boy. Darcy, who had come to stand beside her, made a sound of disgust.

"What? He is a fine-looking lad." Saye clapped Darcy on the back. "Finally figured out how it worked, did you? Well done, Cousin."

"Do not call my son Hey-Ho Henry," Darcy said very emphatically.

"I was not *calling* him Hey-Ho Henry. I was *greeting* him." Saye tilted his head, studying Elizabeth's bundle. "But now you mention it, it does rather suit him, does it not? There is something of Elizabeth's liveliness about his eyes. I think it likely he shall be a loud sort of fellow."

No matter what Saye thought he might become, it could not be denied that Henry was quiet now. The impromptu party swelled all around him, and yet he slept, peaceful and happy in his mama's—and sometimes his papa's—arms.

The Gardiners had also come to see the new addition, and seeing her dear aunt in quiet conversation with

Jane reminded Elizabeth of a long-ago letter, written when she had only just got engaged to Darcy. *'I am the happiest creature in the world. Perhaps other people have said so before, but not one with such justice.'*

And now those words were true again. *The happiest creature, the most contented wife, the most delighted mother... We have been blessed.*

EPILOGUE

On the morning of her fortieth birthday, Elizabeth looked into the mirror and said to herself, "Surely not."

She peered into the mirror again. Was that...? She reached into her curls and tugged, wincing as she plucked a wiry grey devil from her head. Why was it that Darcy only looked more distinguished with the paler, silvery hair appearing at his temples while hers made her look... ragged?

She had once thought forty an extraordinary age, imagining herself rocking in a chair content with her sewing. Hardly so. Indeed, she felt mostly as she ever had, save for those startling moments when she caught sight of a wrinkle or a grey hair and thought, *now how did that happen?*

But no, it was not her encroaching age which had shocked her. It was that only the prior morning, she had felt it. The flutterings and bubbling of a baby in her womb.

Henry had not been six months old when Elizabeth had begun, again, to greet the morning by casting up her accounts in a chamber pot. She had ignored the early signs, thinking that surely, after all those years of trouble, she would not immediately fall with child again. But it was all there, the absence of her courses, the aversion to certain foods, that dreadful taste in her mouth that made her feel she had eaten a horse's shoe. The tiredness as well, but that might have just as easily sprung from the busyness of being a baby's mother.

Oliver Darcy entered the world with ease, and it was an ease that followed him yet, having just gone off to school. He was a charmer, the sort of boy who made people smile just by entering the room. He had little interest in books, but he was mad for sport and games of any kind; fond exasperation was the emotion he most often engendered. He and his brother were both handsome, but Henry was more like Darcy in the sobriety of his air, while Oliver behaved as if he had never had a troubling thought in his life.

And now there would be another. Elizabeth wondered if she had their most recent visit to Italy to blame. Mrs Clark, all those years ago, had found herself madly in love with Nellasperanza and, with all her family gone in England, saw no objection to remaining with him. The two ladies wrote often over the years, with the Contessa Nellasperanza always entreating them to come back and see her. Finally they had, taking the boys with them to enjoy the sunshine and meet their Italian 'cousins', as they had come to be regarded.

"The timing certainly suggests we may have Italy to blame," Elizabeth told her mirror. Then with a rueful smile, she added, "Perhaps if the baby is a girl, we might call her Venetia; it would fit, I daresay."

Jane and Bingley had six children now, all of them boys, and Jane had reportedly told Bingley that she loved him but believed she had well satisfied the duties of their marriage and would stay alone in her bedchamber henceforth. The couple seemed as happy as ever, so Elizabeth believed it likely that her sister's resolve failed her occasionally enough for him.

Her other sisters had been likewise blessed in their family ways. Lydia and Wickham had three daughters, all of them achingly beautiful and shockingly well-behaved given their parentage. Kitty had two sons and two daughters and already occupied herself in fretting over the marriage prospects of them all. Mary had only one son, but that satisfied her and her husband; she was determined her son should make the church his life and devoted her time to persuading the child accordingly.

A midwife had visited Elizabeth that morning, confirming the suspicions she had already known to be true. *A woman does know her own body*, Elizabeth thought; but the opinions of the learned were always good confirmation. No doubt Darcy knew by now and likely had questions, and so Elizabeth rose and went to find him.

It had always been the habit of the Mistress of Pemberley to create a garden of her favourite flower. Darcy's mother's roses occupied a portion of the east gardens, and his grandmother's lilies sat adjacent to them. Elizabeth had created a shady little copse carpeted by lilies of the valley, and Darcy had placed for her a stone bench within it. She found him in her study and invited him to walk with her to it.

He kissed her there before helping her sit, and Elizabeth felt her heart flutter. At forty-seven, he was even more handsome than he had been at twenty-seven. Elizabeth found she quite liked the dignity the bit of grey at his temples gave him.

"It is a bit chilly here still," he remarked.

"Shall you keep me warm?" Elizabeth asked teasingly.

"Do not look at me so, Mrs Darcy. I do not exist solely for your pleasure."

"But I live for yours!" she said with a little laugh.

He chuckled and then said, "I noticed that Mrs Bartholomew called today. Is everything well?"

"Quite well," she told him. "But I do have some news, and it might come as a bit of a shock to you."

"I believe I may guess," he said. "But you want to tell me, and I have no objection to hearing it."

He was smiling broadly, and indeed, it seemed that nothing in the world could please him more than the addition of another to their family circle. Elizabeth found herself filled with happy anticipation as she told him, "Mr Darcy, it seems the happiest family in the world is due for a bit more happiness."

About the Author

Amy D'Orazio is a longtime devotee of Jane Austen and fiction related to her characters. She began writing her own little stories to amuse herself during hours spent at sports practices and the like and soon discovered a passion for it. By far, however, the thing she loves most is the connections she has made with readers and other writers of Austenesque fiction.

Amy currently lives in South Carolina with her husband and daughters, as well as three Jack Russell terriers who often make appearances (in a human form) in her books.

f facebook.com/amy.dorazioauthor

O instagram.com/quillsandquartospub

BB bookbub.com/authors/amy-d-orazio

ALSO BY AMY D'ORAZIO

From the Publisher

The publisher and the author thank you for choosing The Marriage Bargain. The favor of your rating or review would be most appreciated.

You are cordially invited to become a subscriber to the Quills & Quartos newsletter. Subscribers to the newsletter receive advance notice of sales, bonus content, and giveaways. You can join at www.Quillsand-Quartos.com where you will also find excerpts from recent releases.

Made in the USA
Middletown, DE
19 October 2022

13053396R00097